THE COSMIC COMEDY COLLECTION

Halfplanet Press

I0677634

Introduction

Hi, Phillip here. I did have a sweeping, epic introduction to this book, but as it developed, I realised it was in direct competition with the silliness on the following pages. Therefore I swapped out my epic introduction for this more friendly one.

The earliest piece of writing I remember creating was a poem I wrote when I was five years old. I wouldn't read it out loud to an audience again until I was twenty-four, in a Wetherspoons pub in Ormskirk, a short walk away from my university. My audience was Robert Sheppard, my poetry professor and a man with a great sense of humour.

I did alright at uni. I started my own writing society, founded what would eventually be called Halfplanet Press, and began my career as a comedian by reading experimental joke-poems to an audience of fancy looking Arts students. I also consumed enough cocktails to raise the global sea levels by about an inch, which is conveniently the amount of shower water I almost drowned in on the one evening I wasn't partying. They scanned my brain in the hospital, and I quote, "We didn't find anything."

I was also informed I have lovely, thick blood.

My ability to remember the funny things in life, and to give them a higher significance than all those pesky anniversaries, deaths, dark revelations about the cold and unforgiving nature of reality, and birthdays for people whose names I struggle to remember, means that I am biologically biased toward comedy. It is why, after writing all those mind-bending, brilliant, and genre-defining (if not defying) science fiction books and short stories, I still return to the stage to tell people in comedic rhyme how leeches are underrepresented in the media, how I feel about slacktivism, or how I believe the world should be governed after I've had three pints. These ramblings fall out of me at around the same pace the sci-fi stuff happens, and sometimes they intersect.

This puts me in a unique position. I noticed there wasn't much funny Sci-Fi around anymore, and I wanted to fix that, so I wrote some. But just firing it out into the world myself wouldn't be sufficient. So I set about creating this book, forgot about the idea because I had a master's degree to get, set up a comedy and writing podcast, and then found enough authors with a sense of humour to promptly remember the idea in time for this book.

It took a while, but I finally convinced enough authors that they were funny people, and got each of them to write a new story to publish exclusively here. You won't find any of these hilarious tales anywhere else. And, if you are reading this in the distant, post-apocalyptic future year of 2026, and you see some robot vomiting out something eerily similar to this book, please do smash that robot to bits with a large thigh bone whilst screaming, it's what we would have wanted.

And don't freak out when you sober up and find out you've just beaten a real, human time traveller to death, and they look just like you. That's normal, happens all the time. Don't worry about it.

Rawr Of The Wurldz XD

Phillip Carter

Chapter 1

Obligatory worldbuilding disguised as prologue

The alien ship lumbered at the edge of the solar system like a student lumbering in the porch of his girlfriend's house, trying to convince her he isn't drunk. The alien ship also pissed itself and was eating a kebab. It was more of a giant robot than a ship, and more of an abstract, fractal shape than a robot. It was a forever-shifting thing which defied visual description, not just because it was convenient for your narrator, but because it was a shapeshifting thing that survived by adapting to the civilisations it bothered, like a door-to-door salesman pretending to care about your divorce so he can sell you a television. It lolloped and lumbered and stumbled and shimmied about in space, because to fly in a straight line would be more fuel efficient, and would remove the need for this vast hideous thing to hop from planet to planet pinching other people's wesources. Sorry, resources.

Inside the alien ship were some aliens, already perusing the initially commercially unsuccessful films and literature of the little planet they were headed toward. These green-skinned beasties were hungry followers of nostalgic trends and fads, culture vultures hell bent on consuming as much quirky galactic media as possible. Some called them the pop cultists, others called them intellectually dishonest, many of them called them greasy-headed posers. Some called them hipster twats. But always, above and beyond all these nicknames remained their true title.

Invadliens[tm] (patent pending).

It should be known to the reader that the Invadliens were very evil. Owing to the concept of nominative determinism, they had a cultural and almost biological imperative to invade things. It could not be beaten out of them. Not even with a big stick. It was in their nature. Every aspect of Invadlien life, from religion to restaurants, reproduction and science, was based upon the central tenets of Invasionism (not to be confused with Virtualism), their core belief system. When Invadliens were not out invading other planets, they were breaking into their own houses, hacking their own bank accounts, and stealing their own resources. For this reason, their planet looked very much like it had recently been vomited out of both ends of something, for it was in a constant state of theft-recycling.

Having long ago mastered interstellar travel (because they stole it), the Invadliens now sought higher achievements in the cosmos, mainly the theft of brains so that they might vicariously experience the highs and lows of low-tech alien life without the unsanitary risks of sexually transmitted diseases, sexually transmitted religions, or sexually transmitted pre-programmed plot-device nanobots which hide in your sex organs and listen to your thoughts. They're in there. They're in there right now. Get them out get them out get them out get them out get them out get them out get them out get them out get them out get them out.

Anyway, their ship crawled, danced, lurched toward its next target, forever shifting its form to assimilate the rapid-fired memes emanating from the target planet's rich and irony-filled biosphere. The atmosphere was scanned, and presumed to be danker than any dankness ever danked before.

The Invadliens, believing themselves to be gods, wanted only to seek out and experience a life that for them was in the distant past. Their species history stretched so far back in time that to remember it would be to overload the hard drive of the cosmos, also, someone stole all the records. Sure, you can't destroy information, but you probably shouldn't drag it all out of the zip folder at the same time. It's like therapy. We deal with this universe one memory at a time, and the Invadliens deal with their own lost prehistory by sampling ours. It's a form of self-imposed therapeutic gaslighting, or something.

It is important at this point not to start the story, but to list off some random details of the Invadlien species, without which the following tale of their invasion of the monkey planet would have about as much context as that article you just read on the news. Also, I came up with all of this, and it would be a shame to edit it out.

1. The Invadliens are a type 47 civilisation, and are so far advanced that they see the other 46 types as idiots. Humans are type 2.

2. The Invadliens, being shapeshifters, have adopted human form for this story. This not only helps navigate the inevitable budget cuts for the sex scenes in the upcoming television series, it also speaks to a deep existential question about the nature of human existence, probably.

3. Some Invadliens are born with the power of precognition. These ones are often promoted to royalty. You would think that this prescience might permit them some respite from natural chance and predation, but the recent Invadlien king-psychic had no idea I would edit him out of this story, thus rendering this part not canon.

4. The Invadliens are running out of fuel, which for various evil reasons they derive from the molten cores of other people's planets. They also sometimes harvest brains, but this is more

out of habit than out of necessity. It's just something to do on the weekend.

In case it wasn't abundantly clear, the monkey planet is Earth.

They are coming here.

In fact, I think they just landed.

Chapter 3

Unconstitutionally loving the alien

Crawling slowly toward Earth, so as to give us enough time to panic about it and take stylish establishing shots, the hideous, forever mutating starship showed the world its impressive weaponry, most of which was stolen. They had Andromedan claptrap slappers, Extradimensional cabinets (useful as prisons, and for imprisoning Doctor Who fans), Graxxan war dolphins, Mycelial frond cannons, and some other cool-sounding sci-fi stuff.

They also had a plank of wood with a nail through it.

All of which was now pointed directly - or lopsidedly - at Earth.

The first word spoken by the fiends was rough, hardly translatable.

"UwU," said the alien ship.

Followed by a dangerous, foreboding warning.

"XD *nuzzles ur pwecious wesources* XD!"

Then, a single beam of light erupted from the underside of the mothership as it split into countless smaller vessels. The ambassador for the Invadliens had arrived, somewhere in a field in America. One of the fields. It had a tree in it. Probably a rusty truck. You know the one.

This ambassador made his way into the loving arms of the military, who fed him with only their most incompetent staff until a translator arrived. It took several days for the military to find someone able to translate the Invadlien language, primarily because they don't associate with big nerds. The translator, in her mid-30s, wore a Doctor Who scarf and Star Wars shirt. Fearing she might be an actual time traveller due to her aging jeans and glasses, the military put her in her own sealed unit beside the alien ambassador. There was a door between the two, for the Invadlien's convenience, should he get hungry again.

"My name is Remedy Sparks," the translator said.

"Can haz molten coreburger?" the alien asked. He looked Remedy up and down, noting the various pop culture references on her old tweed jacket, and morphed himself to incorporate them in his look. His face became that of Spock from Star Trek, his eyes the roving red beam of the Cylons, and his ears became wide and pointed. Finally, his hair turned blonde and plaited itself like millipedes writhing over each other, weaving itself into Princess Zelda's hair from The Legend Of Zelda.

Remedy Sparks turned to the window of the secure unit and looked into the darkness where she knew the base captain, Jenny, would be watching.

"He seems to be appropriating early 2000s meme culture. Sources indicate that the Invadliens first learned about Earth through Tumblr and Myspace," Remedy explained.

"I'm just glad they didn't catch our first major broadcast," Jenny said.

"Yeah, me too."

"This morning they positioned ships above all our active volcanoes," Jenny mused. "Tell them to back off. We fear they might set off global eruptions."

"Big badaboom," the alien said. Its face shifted briefly to a caricature of Leeloo, from The Fifth Element. Leeloo looked weird with Princess Zelda's hair.

"Nice," Remedy said. She lifted her keys out of her pocket to show the alien a keyring of the water element.

"Wait," a security guard said. He was stood beneath an overhead lamp, his face gaunt and serious. "Tumblr?"

"Yes," Remedy confirmed.

"Could we not... you know."

"Not what?" Jenny asked.

"Convince them they're ugly, make them lose hope?"

"That's disgusting," Remedy snapped.

"Could work," Jenny said.

"It could, but it would ruin our planet's reputation. What if these beings are the first of many? Do we want them to know we are a hateful, spiteful species?"

"They've already been through all of Myspace and Tumblr, it wasn't all group hugging sessions," the soldier said.

"Melody, what does he mean?" Jenny asked. She got closer to the glass, her military uniform taking the interest of the Invadlien, who appropriated a few badges and smiled at the officer.

"Remedy," Remedy said.

"Remedy. Hey! You can't do that," Jenny said, pointing at the alien.

"I can haz war?" the alien asked playfully. It rubbed its fake badges and smiled.

"The soldier has a point," Remedy began. "We're lucky they have latched onto meme culture and not something more harmful like children's television." She turned to the Invadlien. "No ambassador, you can no haz war."

She shook her head and pushed a printed meme across the table to the alien. It depicted an elongated white cat appearing out of the eye of a typhoon, watching over the whole Earth.

"We have a defender, a guardian."

"Longcat..." the alien said.

"The longest and most powerful of cats."

"Can haz how many cheeseburger?"

"All the cheeseburger."

"Cringe."

The alien pushed himself back in his chair. He briefly became Insanity Prawn Boy, from the popular Youtube series On The Moon. After several seconds of him screaming and laughing out the word 'anus', the alien finally calmed down. Now he shifted to a gross hybrid of several characters from BBC's Sherlock Holmes and Supernatural. He snapped one of his fingers off, formed it into a cigarette, and smoked it. The smoke was a darkish green colour, and seemed to move about the chamber with its own intelligence, its own ambition.

"We need to get you out of there," Jenny said.

"Lock me in." Remedy said darkly.

"Why?" Jenny said, even as she gestured for the soldier to follow this order. The young man scurried to the second airlock and sealed it. Remedy Sparks looked out at the observation room with a grim expression.

"I never thought I'd have to relive this," she said.

"Relive what? Tell us what's happening in there or you're getting dragged out of there by hazmats in fifteen seconds."

The Invadlien cracked his neck, twisted his free hand, and opened his palm.

"Would you like a Jelly Baby, Watson?"

Only Remedy knew what this meant.

"We've been SuperWhoLocked."

"What the hell do you mean?" Jenny made sure the airlock was tight, and returned to her position looking into the secure unit. Rather than permit Remedy to answer, the Invadlien took it upon himself.

"Well, it seems there's a preestablished chain of events you want me to see here, some references to 1960's Science Fiction, no doubt. Unfortunately I shan't be able to permit you this delusion as I am presently encumbered by a greater mystery. How does my hair stay so fluffy? And what's more, how does it manage to both woo chronically online females and irk chronically online males? Why does it affect these two groups so differently? And why are the DVDs so expensive even all these years later? That's what I don't understand, but I do understand it, because I understand everything. I am very clever. Also I am very handsome if you're into elves. Which reminds me. Did I ever tell you about the time elves that lived under Gallifrey? I saw one in Dean's hair once. It was totes amazeballs."

"He can't handle three fandoms at a time. He's going to break down," Remedy said.

"And what would a breakdown do?" Jenny asked.

"Well he's copying classic Sci-Fi; any logical contradictions will likely result in an explosion."

"We need to evacuate."

"No, I've got this."

Remedy pointed again at Longcat, the defender of reality, destroyer of TacGnol, the ancient shadow god. The alien did not care for this foreboding symbol anymore. He was chattering madly about mysteries that needed solving.

"That's it," Remedy rooted through her meme folder and pulled out an X-Files meme.

"Lolz. I'm not saying it wuz aliens, but it wuz aliens!" the alien read aloud. His face now shifted to agent Fox Mulder, a much easier character to handle.

Jenny tapped on the glass and spoke into the intercom again.

"Wait. Can we... Can we keep him like that a while?"

Chapter 4

Are there memes on Mars?

After violating several treaties on human-alien contact in the omitted Chapter 2, officer Jenny let Remedy resume her work with the impressionable shapeshifter who, despite being able to sustain a sexual encounter with another species for well over eight hours, just like your favourite Wattpad billionaire werewolf space pirate sex dragon, was not at all tired, and was presently hopping up and down on the table ranting about the old god ChinChin.

"Gib me the core-sy boss," the alien chanted. He was now playing the flute with his nose, and had dressed in a pink morph suit.

"Great, now he's a sex-crazed caricature."

"Not my fault," Jenny said.

"You slept with it."

"Not relevant. Filthy Frank and Pink Guy showed up after the main hype of SuperWhoLock. The alien is learning."

"Oh my god, you're right. He's catching up to the modern day. But how?"

"We gave him the Wi-Fi password," a nameless soldier said.

"Why would you do that?"

The soldier did not reply. Rather, his head opened up and shifted into a foghorn which blasted its horrid sound across the room. His eyebrows knitted themselves into hideous neon green pixel glasses.

"Like a boss," the soldier said.

Jenny made light work of incapacitating him, elbowing the Invadlien in the foghorn face and calling for backup. The room was soon filled with more soldiers and officers, all of whom were quizzed on meme culture, all of whom passed the shapeshifting test when Jenny tried to kick them into increasingly smaller suitcases. It was a basic, rudimentary test, but it worked.

Apart from that one contortionist she wrongly imprisoned.

"We need to get through to the Invadliens, and fast," Jenny said.

"You wasted precious hours on your X-Files fan-fiction lovefest," Remedy reminded her boss, lifting a dishevelled ginger wig up to the window.

"I was trying to teach it how to love."

"And how did that go?"

"It was a bit bitey."

"Right."

"But outside that," Jenny said, "A solid seven out of ten. Anyway, it wasn't all smut. I managed to distract the alien and

14

grab this," Jenny gestured to the large metal doors at the end of the dimly lit room, through which walked two scientists. One of them was holding a glass vial.

"You grabbed some scientists?"

"No, the vial. It's got a microchip in it."

"And where was that on the alien?" Remedy Sparks asked. At this point the alien turned to face Jenny, turning his face away from the pile of printed memes on the table.

"You don't want to know," Jenny said.

"NYYYYEEESSSSSSS," the alien Pink Guy said. His face shifted through various characters, finally settling on Pepe the frog. Finally, the alien sat perfectly still, cross-legged on the table. It began muttering something too quiet for Remedy to hear, and she wasn't about to get up close to it. She had seen enough Sci-Fi horror to know how that ends.

"Ask it what it's doing," Jenny instructed. She handed the vial back to the scientists.

"But who was phone?" Remedy queried the alien. The strange being flickered and mutated, shuffling through various hideous caricatures of old memes. Finally, it vaguely resembled Cell, from Dragon Ball Z.

"Oh no," Remedy said, getting down beneath the table.

"I'm a firin mah lazer! Blaaaarrrgggh!" the Invadlien shouted. But no laser erupted forth from its contorted face. Instead, an eerie silence fell upon the room. Everyone knew something was wrong, but it wasn't clear what.

"UwU, notices ur Invadlien ships. Why u land on planet?" Remedy asked.

"We iz here to glomp ur pwecious wesources! XD" the alien said.

"But which ones?"

"LAVA. HOT HOT LAVA!"

"Got him. I'm calling the Pres, now. We've got all we need," Jenny walked out of the room. Remedy and the alien sat uncomfortably in the isolation chamber, which had yet to be hosed down from last night, and looked out at the soldiers, officers and scientists observing them.

"You're here to take the molten core of the Earth," Remedy murmured. She thought of how to rephrase this in a way the alien would understand.

"We iz Longcat. U iz TacGnol."

"Affirmative Master," the Invadlien said, its head now that of K-9 from Doctor Who.

"How u haz core?"

"Sucky sucky!" the Insanity Prawn Invadlien explained.

A soldier walked through the metal doors to the dimly lit room, putting himself between the others and the isolation pods.

"Miss Sparks. Officer Jenny wishes to inform you that the Invadliens have fired upon two volcanoes in the last three minutes. Our military powers are no match for them. It's up to you now. We need a distraction to get through their shields."

"LAVA. HOT HOT LAVA!!!" the Invadlien said, again as Insanity Prawn Boy.

Remedy racked her brain for something she could use to keep the aliens occupied. She tried one final appeal to Earth's authority over its resources.

"All our base are belong to us."

"No u," the alien said.

"That doesn't even make sense. Wait. Can haz access to ur battle ships?"

"Negative master."

Remedy grunted in frustration. In her peripheral vision she could see the soldiers and officers chatting amongst themselves. Outside this sealed room, outside this military base, outside this desert, the world was ending, volcano by volcano. Invadliens had infiltrated almost every single military installation on the planet, suffocating them under waves of memes and irony. The shitposting and viral cryptocurrency memes had already wrecked the economy, and now the lava pouring down those volcano slopes would wreck the planet, plunging it into a near-permanent winter, choked under ash and the shadows of Invadlien motherships. The lava flowed like a shapeshifter, pouring into towns and cities, melting and burning anything in its path, changing to the shape of the landscapes it obliterated.

That was it. The solution.

"Get me more memes."

One by one, under Remedy's careful instructions, all the world's broadcasting channels stopped talking about the apocalypse and started doing something about it for once. Every transmitter was pointed toward the alien ships, every channel tuned to re-runs of old Youtube Poops and meme compilations. The Invadliens, with no personality of their own, soon became overwhelmed with choice.

Remedy looked at the Invadlien pioneer across from her. He began to shift again, this time into a form she did not recognise from any meme or popular show. This time he was truly alien, becoming his real self. He was a mass of violent barbed tentacles and teeth.

"Shit, they're already shedding it. "Deploy leekspin, eight-hour loop, square aspect ratio, blurry."

"The techno version?" a soldier asked.

"No, classic."

The soldiers turned on monitors in the room, faced them to the isolation pod, and blasted the once-viral video. The Invadlien turned, but didn't seem too interested.

"Reverse enhance," Remedy instructed.

"What?"

"Just smear grease on the screen or something. It's too high definition. It's funnier if it's blurry."

"OMG u filmed this on an iPotato, megalulz," the Invadlien said as the grease was applied to the screen. He was fixated now, utterly fascinated by the low-quality meme.

"Just as I thought," Remedy said, "The Invadliens are not just absorbing meme culture to communicate their intentions with us, they are embodying it. Their predictable invasion of America before the rest of the world, their cartoonish attacks on volcanos. All of this is based on pop culture. They aren't truly sentient, which means..."

"They can be defeated by love and friendship?" Jenny asked, barging through the door.

"Evidently not. No, we can reprogram them."

"My god. They have no culture of their own."

"Precisely. They're grey goo," Remedy picked up a printed meme and wrote on the back of it. "They appropriate anything we give them." She pressed the paper to the glass of the isolation booth.

They'll catch up to current memes soon. And then that's it for us. Make new memes about their own destruction.

Jenny nodded. The military now turned its attention to generating viral content about the Invadliens, resurrecting the ancient memes that had brought them slithering to Earth in the first place. The first meme was tested on the Invadlien ambassador, who was reduced to a bubbling mass of recycled content after being shown a ten-hour Invadlien cringe compilation, replete with completely unnecessary links to a shirt store thrown in every three minutes. After watching his own species relentlessly parodied under layers of dubstep, foghorns, and slow-motion effects, his body simply turned into soup.

This too was added to the ever-increasing playlist of Invadlien cringe moments.

The rest of the Invadlien invaders were defeated through similar means. In fact, they were so busy being defeated they almost entirely forgot to harvest any brains before they imploded. The memes were numerous and delirious, an arsenal that spanned over ten years of pop culture.

Firstly, Earth's Longcat triumphed over the TacGnol of the Invadlien starships. Then Invadliens disguised as Nyancat blasted through their own invisible force fields. After this, the hobbits (Invadlien scout ships) were taken to Isengard (The centre of the sun). To add insult to injury, the survivors were encouraged to shapeshift into the flying spaghetti monster and to entangle each other in a death-knot with their noodles. Back on Earth Invadlien soldiers were isolated and thrust into doomer memes, before being splattered with a very loud metal pipe that fell from nowhere in particular. Liveleak logos were helicoptered in above surviving Invadliens, foreshadowing their hideous deaths.

When only the robotic henchmen and robot butlers and robot sex butlers of the Invadlien species were left behind (action figures coming soon), tactics needed to be changed.

"Deploy philosoraptor!" Remedy demanded.

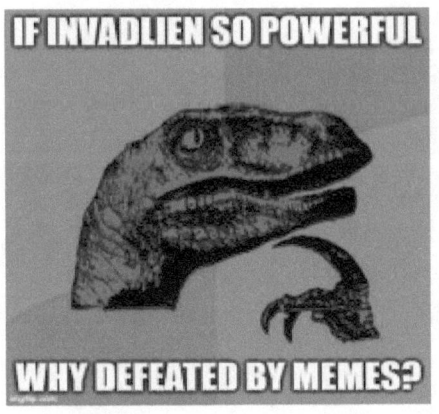

Finally, the robotic remnants of the Invadlien forces were destroyed by the very same thing which destroys that one annoying family member at every reunion you're forced to go to: difficult questions, and also undercooked turkey.

But it was not yet done. The Invadliens had yet more ships on the way to Earth, all of whom had no doubt learned from what they saw unfold there. So, there was one final punch to be delivered.

The world beamed out one final message to the invaders.

"Have u seen Deez?"

To which the oncoming Invadlien ships replied.

"Deez wut?"

Revealing a critical flaw in their armour. It was Remedy's honour to deliver the last line herself. She took to the microphone, leaning close.

"Deez Nutz."

And with that the final mothership exploded.

"Hah! Godeeeeem!"

It was over.

Until the inevitable cash-grab sequel.

Slime Monsters!

John Coon

Bringing the salvaged canister aboard the space station embodied a bad idea to perfection. Doug urged his fellow astronauts to leave it alone. His protests went unheeded. Curiosity tightened around the others with the tenacity of an eagle's talons and refused to loosen its grip. He sighed and shook his head.

No one remembered the curious feline's fate.

Strange alien symbols blanketed the canister. Deciphering the symbols proved impossible. Doug never encountered this language on Earth or among confirmed alien races beyond the solar system. Still, he needed no translator to discern what these unfamiliar words meant. Flashing red lights and blaring sirens would not sound a clearer alarm.

A dangerous unknown substance lurked inside the cylindrical metal container.

"We need to take a peek at what's inside."

Doug snapped his head back at Anna. Limited common sense perfectly counterbalanced her impressive xenobiology skills.

"For the love of God, don't open the canister," he said. "What if an alien bacteria or virus is inside that thing? Exposing our entire crew to a potential pathogen is highly irresponsible."

Anna rolled her eyes, smirked, and brushed back her blonde bangs.

"Don't get in a froth over nothing," she said. "I always take all necessary precautions."

Her assurances did not subdue any troubled thoughts swarming him. Anna entered the lab and placed the canister inside a portable MRI machine. Doug, Evan, and Britt stayed in a neighbouring module and watched a feed from a closed-circuit camera on a laptop monitor. What the MRI scan revealed blew Doug's mind.

Algae.

The canister housed a form of extraterrestrial algae. It functioned as a high-tech incubator keeping the alien organism in stasis.

"Whoa. How did algae end up on an icy lifeless Neptunian moon?"

Anna peered at the camera as though she expected a fellow astronaut to supply a satisfying answer to her question. Evan exchanged puzzled glances with Britt and Doug. He shrugged and tossed up his hands.

"Search me," he said. "Everything about this organism is a mystery."

The abandoned vessel offered no evidence of other alien lifeforms on board. Doug and Evan scoured the compact bubble shaped vehicle from end to end. Their search only turned up the canister. No dead pilot or passengers were aboard the vessel. It struck Doug as odd at the time. An unsettled feeling lingered with him long after they returned to the space station. His eyes trailed along the ceiling as he pondered how an unmanned vessel ended up marooned on an isolated moon orbiting Neptune. Did a larger alien craft purposely jettison the vessel on Proteus, intending to abandon their cargo on the box-shaped moon's surface?

Anna removed the canister from the MRI machine and placed it inside the glovebox. She slid her arms inside attached gloves and started tinkering with the canister. Doug inhaled sharply and instinctively backed away from the monitor.

Anna planned to crack the damn thing open anyway, ignoring his earlier warnings.

"Why won't you listen to me?"

Doug's mumbled question drew no attention from his fellow astronauts. He rubbed his hands through his thinning chestnut hair and interlocked his fingers behind his head. Exploration warranted more caution than they seemed willing to show.

Anna let out a sudden gasp.

Doug snapped his eyes back to the video feed from the lab. The canister lay on its side unopened. It had slipped from the gloves and bounced against the glovebox floor. A fresh crack crossed from a lip near the middle up to the top end.

"Oh God, you broke it," Doug said.

"Chill." Anna shook her head and kept both eyes fixed on the canister. "Nothing is leaking out of the glovebox."

Algae seeped out from the crack and oozed down the canister. It resembled lava bubbling up from a volcanic fissure. The green alien organism paused as though it sensed a foreign presence.

It turned and crawled toward Anna's gloves.

"Did you see that?" Amazement threaded through her voice. "The algae changed direction! I've never seen anything like this."

"Do you suppose it's sentient?" Evan asked.

Anna flashed a grin back at him.

"Sentient algae? Don't be ridiculous."

She wiggled her fingers as the algae drew closer. Britt laughed and pressed a hand to her lips.

"Are you trying to pet the algae?"

Laughter lingered in her question.

"Sure. Why not?" Anna added her own amused chuckle. "I mean, that's the next natural step, right? Since Evan thinks it is sentient."

"We do need a pet up here," Britt replied.

Algae oozed over the nearest glove. Just as quickly, steam or mist rose from the rubber fingers. A sudden sharp scream followed.

Anna ripped her arms out from the gloves.

Doug's brows pulled together and his breathing quickened. He exchanged nervous glances with Britt. All lingering traces of amusement dropped from her face.

This alien organism intended to attack them.

"Get out of there!" Evan shouted. "We need to seal off the lab!"

Algae oozed through the ports. Anna screamed again and floated backward. Her momentum did not exceed the floating algae's speed.

One algae bubble splattered across her right forearm. Another bubble collided with her left cheek and sprayed green droplets toward her lips.

"Seal the damn hatch!" Doug said.

Britt snapped her head toward him. Fear swam through her blue eyes.

"Hell no!" she said. "Anna needs our help."

Without another word, Doug turned and fled to another module. He sealed the hatch behind him, trapping Anna inside the lab and deserting the other astronauts in the neighbouring module. Fists banged on the hatch. Evan and Britt shouted, begging him to unseal the module again.

Doug floated over to a laptop and tapped into camera feeds for every module. Numerous algae bubbles swarmed Anna and settled on her as she retreated into the neighbouring module. Evan and Britt backed up against the sealed hatch.

Anna turned and stared down the other two astronauts. Her left arm lurched forward and seized Evan's shoulder. She clamped down her right hand on his opposite shoulder and pinned him against the floor. Gelatinous green slime flowed from her gaping mouth into Evan's reddened and contorted face. He shrieked and wriggled like a rainbow trout drawn out of a fishing net as his skin sizzled. Lesions formed on both cheeks and along the bridge of his nose. Britt gasped and turned away from him. She banged her right fist on the sealed hatch with greater determination.

"Open the hatch!" Tears streamed down both cheeks. "Don't abandon us, you son of a bitch!"

"You know I can't break quarantine," Doug said. "The algae must be contained."

She clenched her teeth.

"You're a fucking coward!"

Britt wheeled around again and kicked out her left leg at Anna as she drew closer. Anna seized her foot and spewed more corrosive green fluid. The fabric on her shoe melted. Britt screamed again. Anna seized her arm and spit out another massive algae bubble that splashed into Britt's left ear and tightly cropped black hair.

Doug averted his gaze and pressed his hand against his mouth. He fought the urge to vomit. His heart raced like a stock car circling an oval track. That alien organism infected all the other astronauts with minimal effort.

"What do I do now?" Doug mumbled.

Isolating the algae only provided a temporary solution. His instincts pushed Doug to consider much more drastic actions. Quickly decompressing both contaminated modules offered the lone safe option for fighting the algae. Outside of some varieties of microbes and bacteria, few living things on Earth could survive trapped in the vacuum of space.

No. Another option must exist.

Decompression would also kill Anna, Britt, and Evan. Doug stared helplessly at the module floor. His limited medical knowledge offered nothing useful for his fellow astronauts in their current state. Maybe someone else at NASA had a better idea on how to combat extraterrestrial algae. Not that it mattered though. Quarantine policies would never permit him to bring any infected astronauts back to Earth.

What happened in space stayed in space.

"You're only delaying your fate. Your planet, and its abundant water, will soon belong to us."

A distorted and gravelly voice addressed Doug. He whipped his head back to the monitor. Anna peered up at the closed-circuit camera. The whites in her sky-blue eyes had acquired a dark green hue matching the algae.

"We are many," she said. "You will be none."

Green slime oozed between her clenched teeth and trickled out from the corners of her mouth. Doug's face scrunched up and released into an alarmed frown.

"You aren't yourself," he said. "Fight the algae. Fight it until I can purge it from you."

Her eyes hardened into an icy stare. Anna flashed a disjointed toothy grin.

"Your crewmates no longer exist," she said. "We bonded with their brain tissue and absorbed their simple minds. We are many."

Evan and Britt instantly snapped to a vertical position. Their limbs flailed for a moment as though both astronauts were wooden puppets jerked by invisible strings. The same dark green hue overran the whites of their eyes. Gelatinous green slime oozed from prominent lesions where Anna's corrosive slime-riddled saliva landed earlier.

"We are many." Evan and Britt repeated the same words in unison. Both spoke in distorted voices mirroring Anna's cadence. "You are none."

Doug's heart sank as he stared at the monitor. All three astronauts devolved into zombie-like monsters. Drawing out extraterrestrial algae from their bodies required knowledge beyond his own expertise. No choice remained except to destroy the space station and flee on the lifeboat back to Earth.

"You cannot stop us, Rubber Dougy!"

His frown deepened. Anna taunted him with a demeaning childhood nickname. He shared that episode from his past with Britt alone, knowing he could trust her to keep it in confidence. She would have never betrayed his trust in a million years. The sentient algae truly absorbed all their minds, a confirmation that only deepened his escalating fear.

"Rubber Dougy, you're the one!" All three zombified astronauts belted out a song set to an off-key tune. "You make conquering planets so much fun! Rubber Dougy! You're the one!"

Doug clenched his teeth and turned away from the monitor. The damned algae wanted to get under his skin in a metaphorical sense before doing the same in a literal sense. He pursed his lips and shook his head. No chance he'd let an insulting alien organism distract him from the task at hand.

He worked his way toward the airlock leading to the docked escape craft. Doug donned a spacesuit and sealed the helmet in place. Without looking back, he crossed through the airlock and entered the cramped vessel.

Menacing laughter greeted his ears over the intercom as he settled into the pilot's chair.

"We unsealed the hatch," Evan's voice crackled over the intercom. "We will absorb you soon enough. Then, your planet."

"Not if I can help it," Doug shot back.

"You cannot help it," Britt said. "Your brains are too soft and squishy to stop us. We are many. You are none."

Soft and squishy?

Doug scowled and severed the communications link inside the lifeboat. He wished for better final words from former friends and colleagues. Stupid algae-influenced taunts would have to suffice.

Someone needed to toss a wrench into the algae's world-conquering plans. Saving his fellow astronauts or salvaging the space station were no longer realistic options. Involving NASA at this stage only promised more harm than good. Preventing Earth from facing a vicious organism bent on turning humanity into a horde of oozing zombies offered an attainable goal.

This situation called for a selfless hero.

Heroism coursed through his veins.

Doug released the docking clamps and pointed the lifeboat back toward the space station. Solving scientific mysteries gave his life a higher purpose and deeper meaning. He planned to answer a major question with one final grand experiment.

Can extraterrestrial algae survive a collision and subsequent exposure to the vacuum of space?

And The Cat's Dead, Right?!

AJ Pagan IV

Imagine a box, a cage, filled with jagged teeth, part trap, part living enclosure. Titanium alloy covers the eight corners of the box, the walls, serrations. One life could pass through, into the crack, a crevice between, the mouth of the jagged, titanium alloy teeth, curved sharply inward, allowing the soft skin and fur of the animal to slip through, into the box, those same sharp teeth cutting the soft skin and fur and life of the animal were it to try to escape. The alloy impenetrable, nearly uncrushable, unable to be deconstructed safely, its abilities lie in its danger. Trap. Safety. Death. A cat slips in. Meow!

The room was dark grey-blue, the light of the coming day seeping through as the sun's early rays stained by the curtains of old storm. An older man sat at a work bench in his underground lair. Yes, he had a lair, because he was that cool. The man was just finishing typing an email. *I have completed the project! Come at once!* A loud creak broke the silence like a fart in a classroom, the light from upstairs penetrated the depths of lair.

"Get out! I told you not to come down here, Krystal." The man grumped, his sausagey finger clicking enter, sending the email, hearing the whoosh, not realizing that he forgot to include his attachment. With rapidity and a flutter of bio-static shock, he heard the steps of his lair creak and maw with the tiny footsteps. A young girl shimmied over to him, wearing a pink nightdress, tired but smiling, hugging him.

"Good morning, Uncle E."

He let out a breath. He softened at the sight and touch of the little girl, his only companion, and his now legal responsibility. "Good morning. How are you, today? Can I feed you in a bit, darling?"

She beamed at him. "I fed myself. And Dingy."

"Ah, yes, Dingy. How is our little, eh-feline friend?"

"He's good. He really likes to meow."

The old man chuckled. "Mhm. And what was for breakfast?"

"Hotdogs! We each had one."

The old man's face flickered a grin. "The most important food group, I daresay. I hope you didn't have any fruit!"

"Of course not, Uncle E. If I'm good, can you take me to Applebee's for lunch?"

"That's not a lot of time to be good. Maybe for dinner."

"Thank you, Uncle E. Hey, what's that?" The girl was pointing behind the man, at his desk.

The man turned, leering at a jet black weasel, standing upright, a small, weasel sized backpack on the back of the personified animal. The man turned ghost-white. "K-Krystal, go upstairs. Now. Lock the door!" The girl ran up the creaky stairs—or if in Australia, the crikey stairs.

***

A Tomahawk helicopter blasted through the city, blowing citizens down like the Red Light District of Amsterdam, toward Ground One, because zero doesn't count. It hovered for only a second, a black suited body pirouetting from the floating military vessel. The body flipped and twisted as gravity pulled its victim toward the Earth, a series of foam tubes at various cockeyed angles blocking a smooth entrance from above, the body hit and bounced off the foam tubes all the way to the ground. The dark military green mask and balaclava pulled off, a young woman's face appeared. Her skin dark, Indian.

"Wow, I hope nobody saw that." She said to herself, her darting eyes looking around Ground One, a stand-alone home of jet-black looming large against the playground she fell through. "Alpha, you're blowing me to bits. Get the heck out of here." She said into the intercom, the Tomahawk helicopter shot off into the sky.

She looked around, not a single child was on the playground, and she wondered why, and then realized. Maybe it was the yellow caution tape around the playground and jet black house. Maybe it was a school day. And then she saw the people all around, gathering, signs in the air. Chants started. "Playgrounds are for kids!" "Move your murder somewhere else!" LET THE KIDS PLAE! wavered on a handmade sign. The woman muttered to herself as the people walked toward the caution tape. "It's worse than I ever imagined. How did anyone find out?" She spoke into her intercom attached right below her neckline of her darkened, battle ready suit.

A patchy radio response came through. "Hey girl, I think I accidentally sent the coordinates and info to the Home Owner's Association before I sent it to the chopper."

The woman's eyes glowered. "How could you?" She lowered to a whisper. "You know I only rent."

The radioed voice echoed, now booming through the playground. "Well that makes sense given government salaries. Anyway, we really need to find the little girl. She witnessed the murder. I bet these psychos will prolly want to yeet her right out of the house."

The tactical woman shook her head. "Shut up! My heck! You somehow moved from inner ear comms to the fricking playground, you buffoon! And don't talk like that, you are a tactical expert."

The voice echoed throughout the city neighbourhood and playground. "Girl, I don't care if that HOA hears me. I'll cut they dang bushes too short." A series of boos filled the block. Then the people started whispering, talking louder and louder.

Chanting again, the woman strained to hear what they said as she stood in the middle of the yellow-taped off playground.

"We need new signs!"

The woman scoffed. "Jesus, these people."

The radioed voice boomed over the playground speakers. "WHAT YOU MEAN, THESE PEOPLE?"

"Get off the fricking intercom!"

"You best get in that house and solve a murder already. Before they tear yo bootie up."

The woman smirked as she walked toward the house. "No one's been able to do that in a *long* time."

The voice still boomed over the people. "Speaking of tearing up bootie, I've got a hot one on coordinates. Your favourite."

The woman stopped as her hand nearly touched the door handle. "There is no way." The door opened, a young girl, smiling, stood there.

The gritty diesel *WHOOP* of engine growled in the distance. The woman turned to watch the oncoming sound, her gut dropping.

An innocent bystander, not protesting, put his hands to his mouth and shouted. "Dude be getting some, bet."

The tactical woman sighed. "Why is he coming here?"

In the distance, a silver dually pullup truck picked off the highway—wait—a silver dually pickup truck pulled off the highway and forced its way through acres of farmland, ears of corn downed, a watermelon patch decimated (yes, one in ten melons of water smashed and smushed), cabbages ground into the ground to never become kimchi and thankfully, never to become cole slaw—the real devil's lettuce. Thick, black exhaust plumed as the truck tore through and onto the nearest road, sliding sideways, skidding to a halt.

A small, pale man took a four-step ladder down from the ultra-lifted truck, rubber moulded pink testicles the size of rotissed chickens still swinging from the tow hitch. His cowboy boots had three sets of boot straps, his jeans filigree designs only cool people could understand.

The woman sighed, muttering his name. "Brad."

"Yep, that's my name." He stuffed his hands in his pockets as he met up with her near the door. He grinned. "Finally, there's a man in charge."

"Go to heck, you patriarchy sucking fool."

"Is that a slur? Are you just mad I'm gay now?" Brad said as he looked up, the woman towering a foot over him.

"I am not mad you're gay, Brad. I am mad that you are a butthole and treated me like turds, and didn't tell me you were bisexual. At the time."

Brad put a finger in the air. "At the time. Full gay now."

"Yes, we all get it." The woman was exhausted already. "Anyway, want to go in? This girl's been waiting at the door for a few minutes as we watched you destroy some farmland with your really sick truck." She rolled her eyes and stared at him wide eyed.

Brad smiled. "It is pretty sick, isn't it? I've picked up so many dudes just gassing it."

The woman only stared.

Brad noticed. "Don't be jealous. Okay, I think we should go in and talk to this girl. Should have been the first thing you did, Nancy."

The playground intercom came on. "Dang girl, you gon' let him talk to you like that?"

Nancy whispered vehemently into her mic. "Get off the intercom. Now."

As the playground protesters waged neighbourhood war, screaming, chanting, slamming signs and fists into the air, the intercommed voice mumbled softer and finally shut off, transferring to Nancy's ear. "Fine girl, fine, just chill out."

Nancy and Brad made it inside the house, his triple boot straps swaying the way in. A camera no larger than a pinky nail wedged against a picture frame took photos of the intruding duo. Nancy pulled out an iridescent, metallic device, holding it near the nestled camera, watching the screen.

Brad turned and noticed what she was doing. "Oh, you think you're some big shot with new tech, huh? All the tech I need is right here." He pointed at his temple and then awkwardly bent down a few inches, putting his hands behind him, reaching for his massively sized boot straps. The raw leather striped across his hands as he pulled at the third and final strap. "Just these bad boys and the ol' noggin. I'll find out everything, Nance."

She chuckled. "You couldn't find my clit for four years. I doubt you'll find anything here."

Brad folded his still strapped arms. "That's because I'm gay. Plus, how do you think I got into the Government Intelligence Network?"

Nancy's jaw dropped, then she giggled. "They let you in GIN? Are you serious?" Her iridescent scanner pulled up a green and black map ever zooming in, homing in on the camera's transmission location, yet the location kept flipping, switching, they had scrambled the signal like eggs in an easter omelette.

Brad nodded, letting go of his boot straps and popping his polo collar. "Dang skippy. I'm a G-man now."

Nancy nodded. "In more ways than one." Her handheld beeped. Her eyes flickered from it back to Brad. "Wait. Don't you have an uncle or something in the Hexagon?"

Brad walked away, staring at the stairs leading to the basement. "Never mind that. We're on a mission."

Nancy lowered, bending her knees, staring at the little girl. "Can you tell me your name, please? How are you feeling?"

The girl nodded. Her pink cloth nighty tickling her ankles. "Krystal. They took Dingy! And Uncle E is, downstairs."

Brad hustled down the stairs, his boot straps whapping his back the way down. They heard his yell from the foyer. "Yikes! I hope this doesn't happen to my uncle."

"Jesus, Brad. Get ahold of yourself." Nancy hollered, looking back to the girl. "Can you tell me anything else, Krystal?"

Brad yelled again, his voice echoing from the lair. "Yo, this place is dope! Almost as good as my truck. Besides the bloodstains. Gross!"

"Please don't listen to him, Krystal. Brad's an idiot." Nancy rubbed the girl's arm, closing her eyes in disbelief. "Is there anyone you saw, your uncle acting strange?"

She nodded. "I saw an animal. It was a, a, a weasel or something. A real one." Her eyes glistened, staring at Nancy. "With a pack. Uncle E told me to leave. And now Dingy is gone too."

Brad stormed upstairs. "Who's Dingy?"

Nancy shook her head. "Please, Brad, let's focus on the case."

Brad walked over to the pair. "Who's Dingy, Krystal?"

Krystal replied. "My cat. It holds the secrets to the universe. Uncle E gave it to me. He brought it home from Wally World. It's all I have."

Nancy stood up, heading towards the lair, speaking to Brad. "Please keep an eye on her. Actually, you need to call CPS."

The girl's eyes widened.

Nancy made it down the creaky, or if in Australia, the crikey, stairs of the basement. Newly resined, mottled blue-grey floors, lab instruments all about, haphazardly placed, a large, lab coated body, face down on the ground, in a pool of thick, drying blood. Nancy stopped in her tracks, pulling a pair of goggles out of her pack. As she put them on, immediately the room darkened, spotted tracks glowing a vibrant fluorescent green trailed from the left to the right, onto the bench top the man named Dr. Ian T Brill had been sitting at, at the time of his death. Nancy quickly put booties on over her tactical boots, minding the pool of blood, turning the body over. "Javon, are you seeing this?" She said into her microphone.

"Daaaang! That's Syn work. Take a sample at the jugular for evidence."

Nancy grabbed a swab from a kit and rubbed the shredded jugular with it, placing it into a closed solution. She placed the closed kit into a small black instrument from her pack and shut the lid. "Let me know what we get, Jav-

"Viper weasel. And with the camera in the frame upstairs, we're getting led right to them."

"Amazing. But why send a Syn?"

Nancy went back upstairs. Brad had his hands on his hips. The girl sat by the window, watching the protesters yelling to let them into the playground.

Nancy spoke. "It was a Syn." The girl gasped. Nancy looked directly at Brad. "I think we need to go outside. Javon, can you please get someone to take care of this sweet little girl, Krystal?"

The voice rang in her head. "I'll see what I can do."

Brad hadn't moved, his hands still on his hips. "Look. I don't care about the Syn. We need to get this girl's cat back. Now." He planted his pointer finger in a locked position at the ground.

Nancy was flabbergasted. "Wait, are you serious?"

Brad pointed outside. "Let's go. I'll explain."

They walked out of the house, closing the door behind them, Krystal in the house with her dead uncle, again.

Nancy whispered. "I've got a funny feeling about that girl, like she knows more than she's willing to say."

"Nance, we need to save that cat. First off, I just got some intelli that the cat is holding a universe in its—

"What did you say? Intelli?"

Brad looked surprised. "Yeah, what?"

Nancy scoffed. "It's called intel. Or Intelligence. Not 'intelli'. Use words we all speak."

"That's racist." Brad said.

"Okay, no. And just go on with whatever you're talking about, this universe or whatever."

Brad went on. "So I got some intelli that the girl's cat was a favourite of that dead guy. He's a big scientist, physically and in popularity, and he may have planted a microcosm against an antimatter chamber."

Nancy shook. "Seriously?"

"Yes. The microcosm has been reported missing. The chamber itself has a tracking unit embedded, and the last place it was tracked was to this house, which was known. The tracking stopped at the time of his death. Dr. Ian T Brill."

Nancy spoke. "So let me get this straight. The government knew Dr. Ian T Brill had some, super small universe attached to a cat? Wait, how?"

"On the collar, duh."

"Don't you duh me." She said, thinking it over. "Okay, but seriously, this is, like, exactly the plot to *Men In Black*." Nancy said, confusion running over her face.

Brad nodded, smirking. "But they didn't have a sick truck like me."

Nancy rolled her eyes. "You know, if this *was* Men In Black, I could wipe my memory and forget everything about you and that would be amazing."

Brad shot back. "Well I'm gay now, there's no point in coming back to me grovelling, Nancy. You'll never have me again. I'm only allowing men to hold me. And my truck. We need to save this cat. Dr. Ian T Brill was only killed to get to the cat."

Nancy looked off into the distance. "Dingy." Her eyes searched the sky. "Hold on." She scrambled in her pack, rustling, pulling things out, her goggles going back onto her face. She stared at the sky as she clicked the hundred filter options. Softly illuminated fluorescent pink-purple, a small, oblong shape floated in the fog ridden sky. "Brad. I see it. The viper weasel!"

"That's great, but we need the cat. I have my orders, and the weasel isn't one of them."

"Brad! That weasel is a Syn. And that is the reason why the cat is missing. Find the weasel, find the cat. My god, it's not that hard."

Brad chuckled. "That's what he said."

Nancy slapped Brad. "Get yourself together." The playground intercom roared alive again with Javon's jovial, sassy voice. "Ooooo Brad, she got you good!"

Brad wept. "I'm going to call my mom, I can't handle this." Brad ran to his truck, pulled the ladder open, stepped up and hopped into the driver's seat. He tried to slam the door closed but the ladder was in the way, metal crunching, paint chipping. He shrieked, fumbling to kick the ladder and shut the truck door.

Nancy mumbled. "How does he do anything? How is he even." She trailed off.

The playground intercom came back on. "Dat boy got problems."

"Get off the speakers, Javon! Now!"

"Fine, fine. Cool yoself and focus on the case, aight?"

Her goggles still illuminated, she spotted the hovering pink-purple blob, getting farther and farther away.

"Brad! Do you have a gun? A Reacher?"

Brad hopped down from his truck, clipping the ladder the way down. "Ow!" He barked. "Yeah, in the bed of my truck." He opened the tailgate, revealing a score of blacked out weapons of war.

Nancy looked at him, mouth open. "You just drive around with guns in your bed like this?"

"Dang skippy. I keep one under my pillow too."

"This isn't, legal. Or safe." Her eyes flitted to his back window, her head shaking. A giant white sticker across the entire back read *Yeet, Skeet, n' Boogie*. In the corner, a small black flag with a pink stripe, a phrase underneath, *These colours don't run, very fast, but my truck does!*

Nancy scathed. "I can't believe I had sex with you. Even once. Let alone, we were together for four years, Brad. And you're just dumber than, I don't even know. This is surreal. How, why did I do this to myself? And you lied to me for so long. How did I fall for it?"

"Because I'm a catch, and you were falling."

"See, right there! Stupid. Give me the Reacher. Now!" Nancy grabbed for the Specialized Proton Powered Entropy Reducing Massive gun. It was forty pounds and required to be placed on the shoulder. The four inch screen targeted the pink-purple mass. Four red near-quarter-circles locked onto the target. Nancy pulled the trigger, rocking her shoulder, feet planted steadily.

Brad hollered. "Shoot that pussy!" His arms flailed in the air.

She watched the screen as the beam of energy shot toward the target, a half second went by, and the pink-purple mass evaporated into nothingness. The beam kept going.

Brad held binoculars to his face as he declared, "Nancy shot the pussy! Oh look, something is falling!"

Nancy followed, catching the falling object in the screen, a captured image displayed the gravity rider. A metal box, jagged teeth and rectangular slit holes, inside, a tabby cat, possibly meowing.

"Holy heck! It's the cat!" She exclaimed.

Brad screamed. "We need to save the cat! I'll look so good at the office. And the media. We need this! I need this!"

Nancy dropped the S.P.P.E.R.M. gun. "What about this box it's in? Do you have any intel on it? Isn't it supposed to catch the viper weasel?"

Brad replied. "Yes. The intelli says that's what Dr. Ian T Brill was creating. But it seems his creation was the key to his death. And now his own cat is in the box."

Nancy put her head in her hands. "What are the odds the box is strong enough and built with enough padding to save the cat in a fall?"

Javon spoke into her ear. "Odds are fifty-fifty. We don't have all the intelli-intel on the box, but Dr. Ian T Brill's blueprint suggests some sort of gel layer on the interior to keep the viper weasel alive. It's also resistant to heat transfer, which is why you only saw the weasel through your goggles."

Nancy breathed the words, her pulse racing. "Fifty-fifty. Oh heck. It's so foggy, I can't tell where it's going to fall. In the river or on the shore, or."

Brad spoke. "About fifty-fifty. When I was driving here, that corn field bordered the river. I just don't know where exactly it fell from."

Javon muttered into Nancy's ear. "Wouldn't call what homey does driving."

All of a sudden, just as the sun's rays were shining through a patch of fog, the metallic box glinted across the water.

"There!" Nancy shouted, pointing straight at the box, floating on the water, hundreds of yards out.

Brad went on. "I just got a message from G-1 of GIN, the Government Intelli Net. Looks like the box is the most important acquiry."

"Acquiry?" Nancy asked. "What the heck does that mean?"

Brad looked at her dumbly. "Duh, something you need to acquire."

Nancy shook her head. "No. That's stupid, and not a word. And even if it was, improper usage."

"Sure is." Brad said, folding his arms. "But the only improper usage was how you used me!"

Nancy finger quoted the air. "HOW, BRAD? You strung me along for FOUR years! For your mother's sake!"

He ignored her. "Anyway, the box is the most important acquirement. Oh, and they also said don't worry if the cat's dead. As long as we get the microcosm from it is fine." Brad's eyes moved to see a pink dress in the breeze so close to him, he pulled his arm back in fright.

The little girl wailed. "Dingy! Dingy can't swim! Save him! Save him! Don't let my cat get wet! It takes forever to dry!"

Nancy and Brad looked at each other. The media was now only blocks away, large white vans, small black vans, creeping in like ice cream trucks, waiting for the children to run at them. Nancy's deep, galaxial brown eyes, Brad's pale blue eyes stole into one another.

"Ah to heck with their plan." He grunted.

Nancy bent down toward Krystal. "Don't worry, sweetie, my directive is to save the cat, so I will make sure he's back in your hands, safe as can be." Brad and Nancy's directives flipped and flopped like pop rock pancakes.

The girl nodded, Nancy hugged her.

Brad stuffed his hands into his designer jean pockets. "Seems like the cat's about—hold on. Phone call." Brad pulled his phone out of his pocket. "I just want to." He trailed off, looking at his phone. "Fudge. My mother."

Nancy stood up straight, a look was shared with Krystal, silence from the intercom. Nancy looked at Brad, he was grinning as the waves lapped the rocks, the mist evaporated into a sunny day, the protesters screamed and the media vans squealed to a halt. "Brad. What did you just say?" Because, naturally, Nancy heard those words together, more strung along in a loose sentence than one would read said words.

Nancy heard "I just want to fudge my mother." It panged across her brain matter, exacerbating everything that had happened between them. Every moment of theirs shared, each interaction with the person in question. It was horrifying, but it almost, now, just hearing it, nearly, possibly made sense. Nor did that make it any bit better as Nancy thought more and more about it.

Brad put his phone back in his pocket, chuckling.

Javon's voice whispered across the playground intercom. "Did homeboy just say he wanted to... his mom?"

Brad looked up at the large speakers on metal poles, and to the crowd who was now silent. And then to Nancy and her mic. "Wait, what?"

Nancy spoke slowly. "What had you just said, Brad? Because it sounded like." She couldn't finish the sentence, or thought, the words were dragging across her brain like a hot, capsaicin infused rake.

Brad shrugged. "I didn't want to pick up the phone, but my mom's making smash peas tonight."

Javon whispered across the neighbourhood. "Is that a euphemism?"

Nancy cleared her throat. "Anyway! Let's focus on getting the cat in the box out of the water. Who has eyes on it?"

Nancy and Brad, the pair of them used their pairs of hands to grab pairs of binoculars to hopefully spot the cat in the box, floating toward the pair of them. *Brad thought of eating a pear. Mmmm.*

Brad inched forward, his triple loop boot straps swaying behind him, nearly smacking Krystal in the face. She shooed them away as he took another step.

Nancy mumbled. "Retinas on target. About 400 meters out, but it's near a flash tide."

Krystal asked, "What's a flash tide?"

"It's a tide that pulls things out into the Bay. We're very close to the Bay, and it if gets out there, well, then finding it will be a lot harder. I'm calling in a micro-submersible now."

Brad put his binoculars down. "That's not very relevant. What we need is one of those tiny, squirrel jet skis. That way it stays on top of the water. If we pull the cat down, it'll drown."

Krystal spoke up. "I got Dingy after a nice meal at Applebee's with my dad."

Nancy sighed. "Why do you think the sub has to stay under? I'd rather have stealth up to *acquiring* the cat in the box."

Brad was looking at his phone. "This box is supposed to be pretty dang special, a whole lot of new tech in it. Pretty sick, cool, tight if you ask me."

"I didn't." Nancy said stiffly.

Brad turned around, putting his phone to his face. "Going to need an alpha romeo bravo factor force five here in delta.

Roger roger over under." He put his phone in his pocket. "Just ordered a mini jet ski, sucker."

Krystal poked Nancy's black, fitted, militarized suit. "What do you do, Nancy? And is my cat going to be okay? I can't play with it in the box."

Brad spoke. "Probably not kid. That cat's about as good as dead."

Krystal whimpered.

Nancy gave him a look of atrocity before speaking to Krystal. "Your cat, Dingy, is going to be safe. We both just ordered vehicles to safely bring the cat to shore. Maybe it would be a good idea to grab a towel, so you can dry him off?"

"Okay!" Krystal said, running off into the house in her pink night gown, where her slain uncle lay.

Brad looked at Nancy. "Kid said something about Applebee's. I wonder if there's an Outback around here. Want me a bloomin' onion. Share one after?" He asked without thought.

Nancy swooped her head in a gnarly arching half circle. "No. I'm not going back to Outback. Ever. Again. You took me there on Valentine's day."

His eyes softened. "What's wrong with that?"

"Brad, you asked me to marry you. At the Outback. On Valentine's day. With your mom there. The three of us. Right after she sent back the bread for the fourth time. I am never going to Outback with you ever again. With *or* without you."

"Well, fine. Just thought we could share a bloomin' onion." He shrugged, his popped collar touching his ears as he went.

"I'm not celebrating anything with you after this. Actually, I am going to celebrate whenever I leave here and don't have to see you ever again."

Brad scoffed. "Wow, that's like, so rude. Irregardless, I would for sure celebrate this big ol' win with you. But whatever."

"Irregardless is not a word, Brad."

"Oh, really? Why don't you talk to Shapespeare, then."

"Holy cow. Do you mean Shakespeare?"

Brad swallowed, he held his binoculars in one hand. "No." A dark cloud roiled overhead, capturing the sun's rays as quickly as Brad could woof down a bloomin' onion, as quick as the viper weasel slit Dr. Ian T Brill's throat.

Nancy poked buttons on her binoculars. "This is a wild place we're in. Sort of bizarre, isn't it?"

"Oh, now you want to talk?" Brad said, pain in his voice.

"For heck's sake, Brad. Grow up. You hurt me, big time, and then after all this time, after you ghosted me, you text me two years later. A picture. Of you and a guy kissing. It was 2AM. I woke up to a picture of you sucking face with some rando dude, and that was the first contact you had made with me in years after ghosting me. And that was how you told me you were gay. Unbelievable, you are."

Brad spoke, but how he pronounced the words sounded more to the tune of *massage* and *round*. "The passage of time heals all wounds."

"I just can't with you." Nancy balled her fists and shook her head.

"And neither could I. You know, you're a control freak, Nancy?"

The cloud cover was complete, night time threw itself upon the city like a blanket over a nasty woman as the pair bickered like brazen bucking broncos beyond belief as the box bobbed like a buoy in the Bay.

Nancy put her goggles on, illuminating heat signatures and UV reflecting plant matter on the water's surface, giving it depth, sight in this new daytime darkness. "Submersible capturing target now."

"Man! Where the freak is my mini jet ski?" Brad put his hands on his hips.

The tiny submersible breached the dark surface. Four robotic arms grabbed the box, picking it out of the water, liquid draining from the box.

Nancy made a noise. "Heck! That cat might be... wet." The autonomous sub made its way toward shore at four knots.

Up in the sky, coming at them like an arachnid ape on hot Achilles heels, a glowing green orb-like thingamabob floated down toward them, revealing itself to be a parachute with a green light, holding a small white painted, wooden box. Brad opened the box like it was an extra medium snack. A miniature jet ski nestled within plasticized peanuts held it in safety, a plastic model squirrel in the seat.

"Looks like it's my turn." Brad said, hurling the mini jet ski and model squirrel into the water like a football during a football game where a bunch of grown, millionaire men run after said ball and a bunch of poor, drunk, grown men freak out about it. ANYWAY. The jet ski wobbled to upright. Brad used his phone to control the jet ski, the motor turning on, chugging to life, he ripped it to ONE HUNDRED PERCENT.

Acceleration shot through the water, the jet ski humming, zizzing across the water in a fury of speed and ignorance straight at the submersible with the cat in the box floating just over the edge of water. Yards, feet, and inches were shortened in seconds and less.

Nancy hollered. "Brad! Stop! Move the jet—

In a loud, metallic crash, the jet ski slammed into the submersible perfectly head on, bouncing the sub back ten feet, the cat in the box smashing out of the robotic grip, landing in the water once again. The jet ski did not stop after the crash course, the engine still FULL THROTTLE and ripped across the water into the darkness.

Brad sighed. "Well, that didn't work."

Nancy shoved him. "You think?"

Brad moved away from her. "Just gonna yeet itself into the distance. Almost poetic."

She hissed. "What is wrong with you?"

Brad inched his head and squinted his eyes. "Hey! What's—

A small jet-black paraglider swooped down, grabbed the cat in the box and moved up, up into the air, invisible into the darkness.

Nancy rifled through Brad's truck bed of rifles. "It's got to be here." She grabbed a rather skinny, shrimpy looking full stainless steel rifle, shouldering it, standing in the truck bed. She pointed it the opposite way of the paraglider and boxed cat, center mass of the dark cloud. The trigger pulled. Electricity shot out like lightning, a bolt stronger than the will of an ignorant man thinking he's getting some late-night. The black cloud receded, evaporating into the ether. Light shone, rays of golden sun etched across the horizon, the day anew.

"How the frigging heck?" Brad said.

"It's them. They're controlling this. And you're ruining it." Nancy said, hopping off the truck bed.

"What kind of cloud was that?" Brad asked.

"It's called a nano-temp. A cluster of electrostatically charged particles are held in a confined area by the mother drone, and together they draw moisture into a small area, essentially, if large enough, an entire cloud, what we saw here. I missed where the mother drone landed but if we look for it, it'll show up."

Brad put his hands in his pockets. "Don't worry, I'll have it found. My team is coming to clean up as I finish the investigation."

Nancy laughed. "As you finish up? What in the wild dumpster heck are you finishing?"

Brad folded his arms. "The investigation."

Nancy's jaw dropped. "Are you going to steal my work here, then? GIN is not getting this. Sorry."

"We're after different things anyway, Nance. We only want the box. You can get the Synned viper weasel and the creators. And the cat."

Krystal held a light brown teddy bear in her hands, showing Brad and Nancy. "This is Einstein, I call him Steiny. What's a viper weasel? The animal that apparently needed to kill my uncle. Jeeze, what a rough day."

Nancy put her hands on her hips. "It's a, well, a sort of cloned animal that's been harnessed with a bunch of biotechnology and controlled by computers, much like a drone. So it's basically a biologic drone. They created a weasel because it can slip in and out of anywhere and has the hand structure to do pretty much anything. Although that itself could have been enhanced. Be interesting to find out how much tech is pumped in this thing."

Brad finished. "And who's doing it."

Nancy scathed. "Yes. I know that. Anyway." Nancy flipped her goggles on, heat signatures and anti-radar filters seeking out through the limitless blue sky, searching for the paraglider and that cat in the box. "Target acquired!"

Brad replied. "Target inquired!"

"It's acquired, Brad, you sweet little boy."

"You change your mind all the time. First acquire is wrong. Then it's right. You call me sweet. But you treated me like a cigarette." He looked at her, shaking his head.

In the distance, the once jet-black paraglider was now as light blue as the sky, a small attached jet motor pushing it farther up in altitude, a dangling square of titanium box below.

Nancy shook her head. "Treated you like a cigarette? What does that mean?"

Brad looked at her, then to the air, searching for the gliding duo. "Yeah. You pulled me out of my nice little box, burned me, sucked me, and tossed me in the street."

Nancy's eyes enlarged. "Wow. I have work to do. Your little narrative is beyond insane, Brad. And the mother thing. Oh my, don't get me started again."

"Nobody had started again."

"*Your nice little life, box, whatever.* That was you living in a *one bedroom apartment with your mother.* Brad. And I've seen you kiss her on the lips."

Javon boomed over the playground intercom. "WHAT IN THE FRIG IS WRONG WITH THIS BOY? AND WHY DID YOU EVER TOUCH HIM, NANCY? MY GAWD!"

Nancy fumed, stamping her foot and fist simultaneously. "Get off the intercom! Javon, now!"

"Aight, aight, chill." Javon said, half on the intercom, half in her ear.

"What are we going to do about the two getting away?" Brad asked.

Nancy spoke up, her arms flailing with her questions. "Aren't you an expert, in, anything? What are *you* going to do?"

Brad grabbed his bootstraps, in the way a baby would grab for a binkie, he held on, eyes closed, wishing the day away. "Let me think of something. Anything."

Nancy's lips popped in a spark of idea and thought. "We could pull them in with a magnetic retractor beam."

Brad snapped his head toward her. "I was thinking the same thing." He struggled pulling his arms tightened by his boot straps out of his boot straps. "I'll call me men!" He put a hand to his own mic dangling from his shirt. "Alpha alpha tango roundabout, circa niner bee-doo-bop!"

Nancy walked away, shaking her head. "The last thing we need is more men here. And it's *my* men."

Everything quieted, as if in anticipation of something.

Brad whispered. "You don't have any men."

Several seconds later, a burst of noise blossomed through the quiet ruffles of the city, jets blasting between buildings 9/11 style. The HOA cheered for the pilots as missiles glistened and reflected off the sun and into their eyes, UV and infrared alike penetrating retinas, slowly destroying the sight of all who bore witness to the supposed freedom machines cutting the air like a tomato slicer held by a frantic old woman who had too many boxes of unfiltered litter and ex-husbands. The impenetrable mob of jets swarmed overhead, dogging for the cat in the air. A blast of jet stream, the atmospheric one, blew like a Floridian hooker as the paraglider and box tumbled like a rock in a river's stream, all while the media filmed the account live, millions streaming the coverage on dumb phones and telis alike. There's so many streams. The tumbled mass of titanium box and cat inside, the paragliding Syn blew off into the canopy of downtown, the mass of sky scraped by the looming steel and glass as the pack of jets sent missiles hurling toward each building, trying to clear a path for the duo of wanted animals.

Brad put the pilots on speaker. "Romeo Delta, this is Bae-thoven, over."

Nancy couldn't believe her ears. "Did you say Beethoven, or Bae-thoven?"

Brad looked at her exasperatingly. "Look, I get to pick my DJ name. It's Bae-thoven!"

The crackle of voice came through on Brad's chest, his comm system dangling over his neck. "Looks like we got a lot of buildings in the way here. Do we have clearance to use unnecessary force?"

Brad spoke. "Of course, captain. The cat is holding onto an extremely bombastic piece of material."

Silence penetrated the space between them, a slight crackle of imperfect radio white noise came through.

Nancy whispered to Brad. "Bombastic doesn't mean what you think it does. Just say explosive."

Brad nearly yelled into the intercom. "It's explosive, what the cat has is highly explosive. If that cat falls to the ground, it could ignite the core and we could all die."

The jet fighter captain breathed heavily. "Ah jeeze. What are the chances of that?"

Brad sighed. "About fifty-fifty. Just ensure a clear landing zone for the pair."

"FORTY, SIR! We will only destroy the buildings in the way of the cat. Guess we're not having too much fun today boys."

Nancy smiled. "Guess you'll have to go out of country for that."

The jet fighter pilot took that as a command. "We're out of country? Roger that, Nancy! You heard her, boys, shoot those buildings like they're not in our country! Woohoo!"

Nancy rose her voice. "That's not what I—

In the distance, Nancy and Brad watched as downtown levelled. Jets whirred up and over and around, missiles screamed, smashing into glass and steel in front of the still tumbling Syn directed paraglider and cat stuck in the most dangerous box developed in history.

Nancy spoke as smoke billowed, people screamed in the distance, earth rumbled underfoot as buildings continued to topple. "What do you think the body count is?"

Brad shrugged. "I dunno, ten, twenty hundred maybe?"

"What?" Nancy checked her watch.

Brad fisted himself, in the thigh. "Oh shucks, it's Wednesday. I was thinking it was Saturday when nobody was working. But this cat, we have to save it. I mean heck. We will look so good saving this cat and doing our jobs. At the same time."

"You're right. We never get good coverage. It's always wasting tax dollars on missiles and jets and super cool guns, but look! We are using them, and to save this awesome cat. It's a win-win."

Brad looked at her. "I can't tell if you're mocking me."

"I'm good at faking it. But so are you."

Brad jabbed a finger at the ground, staring at Nancy. "I came, once, late, to dinner. I was stuck, in the office."

"Yeah, sure. And I sat with your mom at Chili's for an hour and a half, pretending to have a good time. I just can't even, anything. You're the worst."

"Get over me, Nancy. I'm over you."

"You never wanted me, or did you? I don't even know. The only thing you ever got over was being hung. Remember you asked me to—

"Uh, we can still hear you guys." The jet pilot spoke timidly over the radio.

Brad's face went white. "OKAY! Comms are, funky here." He started fiddling with the comms. "Time to turn you off."

The playground intercom boomed. "I CAN STILL HEAR YOU, BRAD. TELL ME MORE."

"Javon, get off the dang ol' intercom!" Brad exclaimed. "It's not funny anymore."

Nancy cracked a smile. "I mean, that was pretty funny. I'll give Javon that one."

Javon's voice was tiny in her ear. "Do you think the cat's landed yet?"

Nancy nodded. "Right, Brad, we're sadly going to have to take your truck to the landing sight. I guess we forgot about the magnetic retractor beams and just went straight for the bombs. Can you drive like a normal person?"

Brad chuckled. "No! Why would I when I have this awesome truck? You like looking at it, don't you?"

Nancy scathed. "It's horrendous. But I was dropped by—

"By me and a few other guys." Brad finished for her.

Nancy's eyes went wide. "I will assault you if you finish another sentence of mine or add any extraneous detail not involved and pertinent to this case."

Brad shut his truck bed, the cord of rifles loose like logs down a hill, the pink, rotissed chicken sized, voluptuous pair of faux man-meat swayed under the truck.

She looked at him in awe. "Don't you want to strap those in? So they can't fly out?" Nancy asked as she walked to the passenger side of the ultra-high lifted dually and stepped inside.

Brad laughed. "No! What if we need a gun as stat as soon as we could ever need it? And then we have to rifle around for the strap to get to the rifles? That's called being unsafe."

"You really have a way of speaking."

"Thank you." Brad shut his truck door.

The engine started, Brad floored it, peeling out, the four back tires screeching, burning rubber as the slick caught traction, swaying from side to side as they ploughed toward the protesting HOA members. Pedestrians and innocent bystanders jumped out of the way, and unfortunately the protesters also moved, because everyone knows they deserve to be ran over. Holding signs, using their rights given to them by slave owners hundreds of years ago, whew, they ought to die. ANYWAY. The interior of the truck contained one eighty-four inch monitor and painfully bright white patent leather seats. There was no windshield, a camera on the outside live streamed the outside of the truck to display into the truck for the driver and whoever else may happen to be inside. The lag was only one point two seconds.

"What is this, diesel powered?" Nancy asked. "It sounds kind of strange."

Brad smiled. "It's electric."

"Why is it so loud, then?"

"Oh! That's the onboard steam engine you're hearing. Under the floor boards there's a flattened coal powered boiler that powers the steam engine. The engine-generator combo makes electricity, which powers the truck motors."

Nancy's brow scrunched. "Are you serious?"

"Yes." Brad said as serious as he had ever been. "Why?"

"That sounds extremely inefficient."

"What's the difference with any other vehicle?"

Nancy thought. "So, isn't it coal powered?"

Brad loosened his grip on the wheel. "No, it's obviously electric. It doesn't matter where the power comes from."

The suburban nightmare of distant city changed quickly as Brad's truck infiltrated with speed. The monitor displayed heaps of scrap metal and shattered glass, jet fuel covered, intact steel beams, a swat team in a tax dollar pedestrian tank, covered in nano-thermite, towed out a vault from the rubble. People lined the streets, praying for the cat, hoping after all this anarchy and chaos, the cat was safe, the economy, glistening. Brad hit the pedal, Nancy's body crinkling into the white patent leather seat, slipping incessantly toward the floor boards.

"How do you not slip out of your seat?" She finally asked.

Brad leaned up toward the wheel, the crack of a familiar sound hit her ears. He looked at her. "Velcro." Two patches of matching coloured Velcro stitched into his back and pants she hadn't noticed before stretched each bond, he leaned back, Velcro crunching back to comfort.

Nancy looked at Brad. "Brad. What if, they go too far?"

"What do you mean?" He asked, the monitor displaying collapsed buildings and small, still erect ones, a glowing line in the distance.

Nancy pointed to the glowing line.

Brad closed his eyes in agony. "Oh heck to freedom water. I sure hope not."

Nancy pulled out her goggles, the iridescence of pink and purples lit up inside the truck, but the eighty-four inch monitor and camera could not detect what she was looking for. She rolled down the side monitor and pulled herself onto the edge of the opening. A bright glow of a body in the air, a glint of something squarish, heading towards the glowing line stuck out in her goggled view. Even drifting, she had a feeling they'd get there before they did.

The top of the glowing line glowed bright, luminescent green, curling up and over into the openness enclosed beyond. As they ventured closer, the line turned into a wall, lit with green, blue, yellow. A helium and argon sign glowed with the power of sons and suns, for all who could see or read to see. WALL STREET.

Brad whined. "Oh, they're going too far! They're going too far! Dang it."

From the back seat, the little girl spoke loudly, scaring both Brad and Nancy. "My dad went too far in his autonomous car. That's how he died."

They both lurched, screeching. "How did you?"

The girl went on. "There was a bridge being constructed but the car didn't know it wasn't finished and it just runs off of lidar and algorithms you know, so it wouldn't stop because there was nothing in the way. And that was the problem, the bridge wasn't finished so there wasn't any more road and he fell off, the car let him fall off to the ground and that's how my dad died. Now I'm staying with my uncle. Well I guess since he's dead too now I'm not staying with him either. Can I stay with you?" The girl asked, poking the elbow of each Brad and Nancy. "You two are fun. I hope I can live with you two."

Brad and Nancy were still too shell struck to shuck a word into their voice chambers. The rest of the four minute drive was in complete silence. Until...the video monitor displayed an approaching pothole, still several truck lengths away.

Nancy saw it first. "Watch out!"

The truck dropped and bucked as they slammed into the pothole, the bed of rifles metallic-y crashing behind them as they tossed like a gun salad. The video feed was delayed by one point two seconds, so anything in the way was already doomed. Brad slowed the truck for a few seconds and raced off again, shrugging. "It's part of the deal."

Nancy asked, "what about people?"

Brad shrugged. "Part of the deal."

"For who?" Nancy grimaced and turned to the open window, watching a view with zero delay.

As they neared the looming architecture of the meter thick wall, arcing from ground to fifty feet high to ground again over a mile in length, the smell shook them. Urine, cotton candy, ping pong balls and animal must. Peanut shells scattered the street like a fine steakhouse floor as Brad skidded to a halt. They hopped out of the truck, Krystal needing a lift down from Nancy. They looked around, a trifling of pudding thick air hit them as they walked towards the abyss of glowing wall.

A carney in white and red vertical striped jacket approached them, holding a veil of fine, iridescent poly open, covering top to bottom, WALL STREET, which only allowed the wall and sign to be visible from the outside. "Tickets, get your tickets. Bears fifty. Bulls two-twenty-five."

Brad looked at Nancy. "Should we bet on anything?"

Nancy ploughed through, moving toward the raucous ongoings in front of them. "We have a cat in a box to find, not sure if it's dead or alive, and a viper weasel. That's bet enough." She showed her badge to the carney.

The carney shook his head. "We only have the finest purebred corporate animals here, darling. Syns are not welcome here. No rules about cats, though. Here." He allowed them through.

Nancy kept walking, Krystal running after her.

The blue sky did not shine here, as WALL STREET was too murderously high and black-holeish to allow light from any object to shine on these activities, here.

Brad whispered worriedly as they went on, under the veil of WALL STREET. "Nancy! Don't you think they floated onto the veil and slid down the side or something? You don't think they're actually in, here, do you?"

They found themselves at stainless steel animal stalls, black bears and grizzlies in confinement—feeding on corn and the blood of felled tenants—sitting in the shadows, tongues lapping the ruby liquid as hoarse breaths covered Brad's whispers. Thick padded feet silently moved the bulky animals as they moved from corn and blood liquor to piles of cash, nestling in to burrow for the long, capital winter.

Nancy broke her stare, snapping out of it. "Brad. I think the viper weasel is smart, most likely smarter than you. And this is a great place to hide. It probably cut through the veil and is hiding in here."

Brad moved toward her, they were face to face, nose to nose in the darkness. "You think they're hiding in one of these bear infested money pits?!"

"Possibly. Easy to hide plenty of things in here." She reached for her pistol. "Come on, let's check the bull pen."

And a rodeo it was. Bulls, with the musculature of Michelangelo's David and the finest Belgian Blues, with a mutated gene for myostatin, the bulls were as strong and ripped with muscle as any animal or human could ever be, making Arnold Schwarzze-something look like a fat lard in a loose sausage casing covered in butter. Carneys lined the pens, screaming, tossing paychecks and mortgages at the bulls, corporate brands seared into the buttocks of the horned and hoofed animals. The bulls chewed the cellulosic bills, growing, earning, each bull was weighed, measured, inspected by a hundred men, yes men, only men could ever possibly do such a glorious, important job! They screamed and shouted, giving, dumping truckloads of funds, a hedge, ten, twelve feet tall covered the back wall, as verdant and vibrant green as a hedge could ever be funded with manure and fertilizer and cash. Men, millionaire men, billionaire men, in shirts with words TOO

BIG TO FAIL poked and prodded everyone at bay, shouting, red in the face, to give money to their bulls, to feed them, make them feel anything at all.

The girl pointed toward the hedge. "Is it, are they in there? The bush?"

Everyone stopped, looking at the little girl. "IT'S A HEDGE!"

Nancy responded to her. "Possibly. Let's keep looking though."

They went on, the loud men with hot pokers, collecting fibres of currency to keep the bulls as muscled as ever. A small pen, one off to the side caught Nancy's attention. A placard above in bright white letters glowed for all to see - CHAPTER 12. A bull, as skinny and frail as a ninety year old woman about to see nothing forever after, bones and skin as limp as dried herb, sat in a rocking chair, an IV of gold nanoparticles dripping in to nourish the once-fine animal. The caretaker walked towards them. He pulled a stethoscope off his neck. "Would you care to help this poor company out? Their finest bull is near the slaughter. Anything will help. We have debts to pay. We've collected all we can. We've taken back all our rentals, all the homes in our portfolio. We just, we need help. Even the government stepped in, but still, we need more. Or this old corporate cow will die."

Nancy looked at him straight faced. "And what did you say was the market this company was in?"

"Rental properties and mortgages." The caretaker said. "We evicted all our tenants and bulldozed the homes, we tried to make a mall, bring in the white people, still, it didn't work. Where did we go wrong? Do you have anything to spare?"

"No." Nancy walked off.

Brad wiped away a tear. "Nance, please, Nancy. They're just, trying their best. Look how frail this company is. Just look at it. They don't have any more boot straps to pull."

Nancy looked at Brad. "You've got a few to spare." She walked back over, the limp, skin and bones bovine's IV was nearly up. "I literally do not care. I have a cat to save."

The caretaker shook his head. "Pussy." The old bull fell out of the chair, tongue lolled out of its mouth. The old man put his fist in the air at Nancy. "You killed it. You killed it. Shame on you."

They moved on, searching for any rip, tear, mend in the veil of WALL STREET above. For any place a weasel could hide a box that could hold itself, or in this case, a cat.

Krystal asked them both, bewildered. "What is this place?"

Nancy took a long breath. "This is where companies place their bets. They fight them. In the same ring. One bear, one bull. Same company. If the bull wins, they make a lot of money, and they stay bulls. If the bear wins, they lose money. And if the bulls don't make as much as all the others in the room think they should, they also become bears. And that's about it."

"What a strange place." Krystal said. She grabbed Nancy's hand. "I miss Dingy."

Brad pointed to the main event, the *Bear and Bull Corporate Rodeo Showdown*. He led the way, through the tens of scores of people with gilded shirts and shoes, prostitutes and parachutes. "Yeah, kid. We'll find her. Sooner or later, we'll get your cat."

Krystal looked at Nancy for approval. "But Dingy's a boy."

Nancy tried to console her. "It's a matter of time."

Brad went on. "I'll bet fifty your cat's in the ring."

Krystal muttered. "My cat in a box, in a ring, on WALL STREET. Where does it end?"

Nancy chuckled. "Dingy will be in your arms soon. I know it."

They made it to the main event, beggars and hopefuls in silk suits lined the arena—a giant, bubble gum pink, opaque and oblong bubble, nearly thirty feet high, sixty feet in diameter. Inside, the four corners of rodeo ring were made of raggedly chopped wood, only two thin logs per side held the beasts at bay. Millions, thousands, tens of dollars worth of bonds and stocks and bills floated in the air of the bubble and scattered the floor, milk spilt by government workers leaked in the from the far corner of WALL STREET gave the putridly sweet smell of sickened lust. Five inch long fur, shaggy and thick with swagger, black as night, yellowed teeth, paws as large as small dinner plates, a crimson red cape covering its back, a black bear stood on hind legs against cedar logs. In the other corner, a thick, squat, portly yet also jet black animal, a wagyu bull, as fat as could be, with sharpened horns of keratin refused to be killed with the swat of a bear's paw before a long corporate winter. Cash dumped from a drone above, a thin, iridescent dump truck bed of the drone poured the green bills faster and faster, raining on the furious animals as they shared tooth and hoof, claw and blood. The drone tipping still, something in the back stuck to the dump-bed of the hovering device, and slowly, it slid. The people noticed.

"Look! What is that?"

"Is it a bird"

"Is it a plane?"

"No! That doesn't make sense."

"Nor does a bird!"

"You mean neither."

"Or either, they both work! All three, threy? Is that a word?"

"Is it a—wait, it's a box!"

Nancy exclaimed. "It's the cat! Look!" She pointed, Brad catching the sight as the box tipped from the drone, head over heel, top over bottom, the metallic, jagged toothed box filled with fluffy little animal inside turned as gravity took its toll. It hammered down flat onto the arena floor of dirt, a cloud rose in between the bull and bear.

Brad looked at Nancy. "What are the odds of this going well?"

A hundred people leaned in. "Fifty-fifty!"

"Two to one hundred!"

"Fifty to one."

"One to fifty!"

"Seventeen?"

Brad shook his head as he looked to Nancy. "Just a little Brian-in-a-box, that poor kitty can't even move on its own. It can't use its legs, just waiting for us to do something about its life. It's sad."

"I think you mean 'brain-in-a-box', Brad." Nancy corrected him.

Brad huffed, shaking his head.

9AM struck the clock like anyone should a red headed stepchild. The animals tore into each other, growls and guttural screams commenced as the animals became silent in fury, fighting to the death for corporate future. The bear swiped down as the bull's horns hooked up, the boxed-cat inside, right behind the back left leg of the bull. The heavy bear's paw came down onto the bull's head, slamming into skin, skull and brain with the ferocity of a goddamn bear swiping into anything at all. The bull dropped cold, back legs flicked out from under it, kicking the box Nancy and Brad and Krystal were hoping to grab, up, up and out of the ring, slowly, quickly, oh it was a horrendous show in slow motion as all watched the sharp metallic corners of the box glisten in the light of the fiery arena as it neared and caressed the edge of the pink bubble. The bubble stretched like a kid chewing gum, farther and further stretched, the box nearly ensconced in pink bubble kept going.

And that bubble POPPED! The crowd went wild, screaming, calling in their bets, falling over, medics rushed in with gold nanoparticle IVs quicker than rice pudding or EMTs in a ghetto. The arena was a madhouse, Brad, Nancy, and Krystal caught in the calamity of a corporate bear market. The red caped bear broke free of its arena, running after investors, swiping paws, claws and teeth, tearing into them left, right, and centre. The heyday was not a helloday, chaos reigned as people screamed and fought, the red caped bear, named EmNom, ran through and over investors, breaking free the stainless steel corrals of hibernating bears. Bulls ran the streets, searching for cover just as human searched for cash. Blood curdling screams were heard from all over. "MY 401k!" "ROTH IS DEAD!" "THE ECONOMY!" "MY THIRD LAKE HOUSE IS RUINED!" Nancy grabbed Krystal's hand and followed as Brad ploughed through the crowd of sobbing millionaires, using his boot straps to clear the way, leather whapped and slapped toward the still flying cat in the box.

WALL STREET was in shambles. The veil was torn, rippling in the wind, investors covered themselves like a naked woman in a window. Horrified that the regular, poor people could see inside, they screamed, cried, this wasn't supposed to happen again, and again, and again, and again. A river of tears formed through the city streets like a burst levy. Nancy acted fast, pulling out her First Travel Kit, rummaging through the foldable bike and chair to reach the inflatable kayak. In an instant, they were all inside the poly kayak, floating down Main Street as the reinforced jersey walls on each side had kept the HOA protesters inside, and away from safe, normal people, minutes before. The barricaded Main Street was moving North, and like the Nile, a constructed waterway because natural water can only move South. Pollution filled the flooded street, signs catching on jersey wall seams and chain link fence, a bright pink sign with faded marker read:

PLAYGROUN-

D 4 KID!

Krystal spoke uncomfortably loud against the havoc. "Where are we going?"

Nancy had her spectroscopic goggles on, viewing the sky for the box, the viper weasel, any sign at all. "There! No longer in the sky, we have a solid chance. Brad, do you have a motor or anything?"

Brad replied. "No. We just need a motor on this puppy and we can grab that kitty!"

"Yeah, that's what I said." Nancy shook her head. "We're only one hundred, maybe one-twenty meters from the target."

Brad was taken aback, shaking the small, inflatable kayak. "What the heck does that mean?"

Annoyed, Nancy replied. "Don't you know what a yard is?"

"Yeah, of course. Don't woman-splain it to me."

"A meter and a yard are a few inches off. Ten percent."

Javon spoke loud enough through Nancy's comm system, Brad, Krystal, and anyone around could hear. "Brad should know what a few inches off is like."

Nancy cracked a laugh, holding the rest in. Her face reddened as she turned around, Brad fuming against the yellow poly.

He spoke. "Real funny, Javon. And where the fiddler's heck have you been?"

"I went to the bathroom, mister sassy." Javon went on, the crackle of the comm crackling like cracklings in a vat of fat. "You know, that place where you pee. Sitting down."

"Okay then. We do have a kid present." Nancy saved Brad just a few little inches too late.

Krystal spoke, her voice as soft and hopelessly sad as ever. "Nancy, will we ever get Dingy?"

Nancy turned around in the kayak, Krystal in between herself in front, and Brad in back. "Of course. We're almost there."

Krystal's face lit up. "I can see them! I see Dingy!" She pointed down the riverine road, a red raft upon which a slick black weasel held an automatic weapon, a silvery box with jagged holes behind it.

Nancy pulled out a small electronic device, pressing the only button on it, a large, bright purple button, labelled ON. A holographic display lit up from the device, concave lines gridding out in front of them, vision was distorted blue-purple within the large circular area like a giant, electric contact lens.

And not a moment too soon, as bullets flattened and dropped at the energy shield Nancy placed in front of the kayak. The viper weasel fired at the enemy combatants. Brad whipped out a pair of silver pistols, handing one to Krystal to hand to Nancy.

Krystal held the gun for a moment. "The last time I saw a gun this close, I was in school."

Horrified, Nancy turned, carefully grabbing the pistol from the little girl's hands. "I am so sorry you had to deal with that Krystal, but we have another situation in front of us. Let's talk later."

"The news called us cowards because we don't want to get shot in school. Can I bring that in for show and tell? I'd be the coolest kid in school. And then maybe the news would stop making fun of us."

Nancy pushed Krystal to the floor of the kayak. Another shot rang out, a bright patch of red and orange popped in the energy field, the grey-black mass of flattened bullet fell into the river of tears.

Brad shook his head. "Man, I wish I had my truck."

"What for?" Nancy yelled, as she aimed her weapon, firing at the incredibly small target of a weasel at fifty meters, fifty five yards for Brad. The raft popped, enveloping the titanium box with cat inside, sinking slowly, the weasel nowhere to be seen. "Christ! I missed. What are the chances?" The flooding increased, water rapidly flowing, surging like troops in a failed war.

"About fifty-fifty." Javon said over Nancy's comm.

Brad shot at the water, loosing an entire clip into the saline mass.

"Stop!" Nancy yelled. "If you hit the microcosm, we could all die!"

Krystal cried. "No! Don't shoot Dingy!"

Brad scrunched his face. "Oh! Why'd you have to tell the kid where I shot!"

"Did you shoot the cat?" Nancy asked, half bewildered, half scared, half shocked.

"NO! Shoot! But when I shot, I think I missed a shoot or two and now it's all shot. I need a magazine."

Krystal wiped her eyes. "Uncle E liked to look at magazines with naked people in them."

On the other side of the jersey wall, a toga wearing, dark skinned, Arab hippie with sandals and long hair called for them. "I heard you call my name, Nancy."

Nancy shook her head. "No. I didn't. What do you want, Jesus?"

The man gripped the fence like Border Patrol was nowhere to be seen. "Just your soul and everlasting love."

"No thanks. That's weird."

The hippie's eyes softened. "How about belief in me, Nancy? It's been so long. I can give you health care and food. Care for each other. No country or company can do what I do."

Brad looked from Jesus to Nancy in horror. "Oh my god, he's a communist! He wants to give us food and medical. We must declare—I can't believe I am going to say this. But we must declare war on Jesus!" Brad grabbed his radio.

Nancy put a hand to Brad. "Just hold on! We can only declare one war at a time. That's what we do. We mess one up, wait too long, hope people forget, and then start another. Just wait. We have this dang weasel so close to us. Jesus can wait!"

Brad's phone rang. Another shot hit the energy shield. And another. Brad's phone rang again.

Nancy turned her attention away from Jesus—thoughts and prayers and all, toward the active shooter. Bobbing just at the surface, she saw the faint outline of the weasel. She aimed carefully.

Brad yelled. "It's my mom again. I have to pick up. What's up, mom?"

Screaming on the other end. Nancy's full attention was pricked and pulled and separated like a newborn's circumcision.

Now it was Nancy's turn to yell. "Goddangit! Shut your phone off, Brad! I missed the shot again."

Brad turned his phone to speaker mode. A woman yelled from the other end. "And then they wouldn't take my trash. Like I wasn't good enough. So I said I need to speak to the manager, and they called the police on me! Can you believe that? So now I need you to come down to the police station, my ittle wittle Bradly. Can you do that for me?"

Nancy heaved so hard she almost vomit. "I do not miss that voice."

The phone snapped. "Who is that? Oh, that brown girl you dated, isn't it?"

Nancy hiccupped. "Brad, if you don't leave your mother in jail, I might have to kill you."

Brad turned red. He whispered, "I don't know what to do."

As the enveloped cat and viper weasel was ignored by the team so close but so not close enough to get to, the phone went on. "They want me to sit on this metal, thing. And I just can't do that. I have had a bad back, that idiot doctor gave me those pills, but not enough! I only needed a few more bottles. And I haven't seen you in church as of late, Bradly, and that's the only thing to redeem you in our hearts. I mean god. But anyway, you really do need to find a woman and forget that awful lifestyle of yours, it's an embarrassment. And you know, this isn't the first time they tried some bull with me at that coffee shop. That girl might be in high school, but I told her last time, if she didn't quit with the act, I might have to beat her like I did you."

Nancy grabbed the phone. The woman, Brad's mother, had legally changed the spelling of her name from *Karen* to be cooler than the average tool, pronounced the same, but with that white-girl jive and existential crisis one would need to be such an effin' loser. "Kyryn. Nothing would make me happier than to hear about you going to jail. But right now we have a situation that I need to control. So we're hanging up. And maybe you can rot in there. Oh, and Brad declared war on Jesus."

Screech! Nancy hung up, tossing the phone to Brad. "Just have some balls, Brad."

He snapped. "I can't hang up on my mother! How could you say that about Jesus!"

"You did! It's time to stop pretending to your mother, you're a grown man, kind of. Help me find this weasel and quit the other junk already."

"Fine." He hissed, his brow sweating, already thinking of the next time he sees his mother, scared to no-wits start.

They looked on as they floated down the billion dollar stream of tears.

Nancy bellowed. "HOLD ON. WHERE IS THE CAT?"

Brad scrambled to put his goggles on, he let go too quickly, the strap snapping back, slamming against his nose. A small, red-purple body twisted and turned under the water's edge, grappling against the grey-white raft and an outlined box in infrared vision. He hollered. "They're—

Brad was yanked by the neck, his body smashing into dry concrete and asphalt. "What the heck was that?" He exclaimed, pulling his goggles off, coughing.

Nancy huffed. "Had to. Waterfall." She put her hands on her knees. Then pointed down. "I really hate this city."

Brad stood up, Krystal staring at him. "Hot dog!" He said. "The luck to have such a woman man-handle me, save my life."

Nancy blushed. "Enough. For whatever reason, we're on this case together. I am legally obligated to save your life if need be. Let's go around. Can you call your truck?" As she rung out the salt water of her black tactical pants.

Brad put on a fat grin. "Nothing would make me happier than to call my truck." He put his hands to his mouth, rose to the sky and hollered as loud as he could muster. "Beep beep boop tonka tonka!"

Nancy stared at him. "What the heck was that?"

Brad looked at her in all seriousness one would after calling for their autonomous, coal powered, electrified dually truck. "That's my truck call. How you get it back in the wild." In two instants, instances, the silver monstrosity came ploughing forward, people dodged out of the way as the truck fjorded the river of tears from the other side, ramming across, heaving, chevving, ro-leying toward them. A thick black plume of coal dust shot out from the back of the man machine as it skidded to a halt, Brad put a hand across the hood, gleaming, grabbing his four-step ladder to step inside, his boot straps swaying as he stepped higher and higher toward paradise as all the people of the world ooed and aahed as he got inside. And then he snapped out of it. The eighty-four inch monitor was cracked on the driver's side! A large jagged line seeping black death reeled across the screen.

Brad heaved, mumbling, whispering. "Armageddon."

Nancy helped Krystal in, hopping in herself after.

Krystal pointed. "I bet it was the weasel!"

Nancy looked in the back at her. "Nice work, Krystal. It could be. Let's find out."

Brad shook his head, a quick look through the rear-view monitor. "This kid is creepy. I gotta yeet her out my ride. Come on, kid. Scat, like a bear."

Nancy smacked him in the chest. "You will not abandon this child! We have a responsibility to her."

Brad shrugged. "Can't someone else? It's rather inconvenient she's here."

Nancy fumed. "She is a witness of a murder and a child, Brad. You can't just abandon people. Wait. That's what you've always done."

Brad rolled his eyes. "Here we go with the gay thing again. I'm not interested in you, Nancy. Okay? Just believe me. I don't want you anymore. Guys only. Big guys with cute trucks. But I can only ever find small guys like me with big trucks. What am I doing wrong? Nancy? Nancy?"

The truck door slammed. And the back door opened. Nancy unbuckled Krystal's seat belt.

"Brad Wilder Caucusatonian, you are officially relieved of your duty."

"I sure ain't be!" He jumped out of his truck, a mere two seconds went by before his boots touched pavement. "Look. I'm sorry. I didn't mean it about the kid. It's just, my mother. She's nuts and it really bothers me and I'm putting it on the kid. I'm sorry. Krystal, I'm sorry. I will protect you."

Krystal nodded. "Can we be a family now?"

Nancy's jaw dropped, head cocked like a rooster. Krystal put her arms around them both.

"My new mom and new dad."

Nancy's body shook. Javon cackled laughter in her ear. "Ahahahahahaha! This kid wild! I love her!"

Nancy pried Krystal's arm away. "Sweetie, look. I will protect you. For now. But someone else will have to take care of you as you grow up. Do you have more family?"

Krystal nodded. "Yeah, just follow the weasel."

Nancy's face turned stone cold like a rock in the Rockies in winter. "You know whose weasel that is?"

Krystal nodded. "Yeah, my other uncle. They were best enemies."

Brad put his hand to his head, confused.

Javon went over the truck speakers. "For real? This kid something else."

Nancy snapped. "Javon, get off the speakers!" She kneeled down. "Okay, Krystal, can you tell me where your other uncle lives? What's his name? Any info at all?"

Brad nodded. "Any intelli will help, kid. We're here for you."

Nancy huffed.

Krystal looked at them. "Promise to be my new mom and new dad?" Her eyes brightened, glowed, growed—grew three times as large as she stared at the bickering pair, a smile lighting up her face.

Nancy deflated. "Yes, I promise."

Krystal beamed. She looked to Brad, and then out in the distance, to the water, across the way, the jet black house and the playground with abandoned, mispelled signs. She pointed. "That way. The weasel will go that way and then we'll find him."

Brad put his hands in the air. "I knew it! I knew this kid knew something! Dang it to heck, I should have put a bet on it."

Nancy stood up, speaking, looking at Brad for a split second. "All right, let's go. Brad, roll all the monitors down so we can see out of this stupid moving thing you call a husband."

They hopped back in the truck, the monitors rolled down, their heads out of the windows, the crank of the onboard coal generator rumbling as the electric motors streamed in silence.

Brad pointed into the air as he ripped the pedal. "I see them! There their!"

Nancy scoffed. "Okay, did you say 'there their'?"

Brad nodded. "Yes. And do you see them?"

Nancy looked up, noticing the paraglider again, going in the opposite direction of the jet black house. "Yes! I see them. But we need to work on your spelling. It's 'they're there.' Not 'there their.'"

Brad shrugged. "How do you know how I'm saying it?"

"I just can. I know how dumb you are."

He shook his head. "My mom says that to."

"There it is again! It's *too*, not to."

"Yeah, yeah, the two twos."

"Oh my heck! First off, there are three spellings of what we're talking about. 'To.' 'Two.' And 'too.' Do you understand?"

Brad pointed. "Nancy, do you understand there are more important things than to just correct me all the time?"

Nancy begrudgingly agreed. "How are we going to get them now? This weasel is dang crafty."

Brad looked back at Krystal. "All right, kid. What's going on? Where are they heading now?"

Krystal smiled. "Let's go to Olive Garden! Since we're a family now."

Nancy's face reddened. "Krystal, do you really know where they're going, or did you just say all that to get us to take care of you?"

Krystal smiled, shrugging. "I want bread sticks and a blooming onion."

Brad corrected her. "That's at the Aussie steakhouse, mate." He looked to Nancy. "Remember how amazing it was?" His smile as wide as his truck stole her vision.

Nancy put her head in her hands. "Something sure was. Like my ability to see nothing. How can we capture this weasel? Bait?"

Brad nodded. "Yes! Bait. We need a good one, a best one, a master baiter for this sort of job. We've already gotten our hands dirty, we need a professional before the mess comes everywhere."

Nancy shook her head. "You've singlehandedly had downtown levelled. WALL STREET's bubble burst, into a River of Tears no less, protesters ran rampant as we got here because a playground was closed. When and what would you then define as a mess everywhere?"

Brad furrowed his brow. "I'll think of something."

Nancy heaved a breath as they watched with binoculars as the paragliding weasel flew high and mighty, wearing a tiny backpack, a cord and clamp attached to the titanium box, cat inside as the truck sped through the crumbling mess of city. "We're going to need my helicopter back. Javon!"

Nancy's comm lit up, a heavy, garbled voice huffed over the intercom. "What now? I'm busy."

"Again? What the heck are you doing?"

"It's lunch time, I'm eating vienna sausages and peppermint sticks."

Brad oooed. "What flavour?"

Nancy cringed.

Javon answered. "Buffalo, of course. And peppermint."

Brad replied. "I like mine baked."

Nancy cringed twice in a row.

Javon sighed like a night train coming down on a pack of New Delhi cows. "Typical."

Brad retaliated. "What in tarnation is that supposed to mean?"

Javon ignored Brad. "Nancy, chopper coming at you fools in three."

"Bravo." Nancy replied. "I'll move to the bed." She started mumbling. "With all the loose weaponry."

Two.

One.

The helicopter swarmed overhead in a flash, dark shadow and blades chopping, splaying, whooshing the air.

Nancy looked up. "I thought you meant three minutes. That was three seconds!" She moved her way into the back of the truck, Krystal staring at her. The back monitor opened up, Nancy shoved herself through.

Javon giggled. "Yeah, but you're with Brad, you should be used to that."

Brad sighed.

A robotic voice bellowed from above. "Stay where you are. Wait. Be seated. Install belt into seat. Repeat. Stay where you are. Wait. Be—

Nancy yelled into her comm. "Javon, what the heck is going on with the Tomahawk?"

Javon giggled. "They have a mind of their own. Autonomous vehicles are the worst, aren't they?"

Nancy stared at the helicopter as it followed straight above them, a giant cable and magnet dropping from the bottom of the chopper. She pulled herself back inside as quickly as possible.

BOOM!

Brad screamed in italics. "Ahhhh! My truck!"

As quickly as the magnet and cable fell, the truck lifted from the ground, hovering, wrenching upward on the Tomahawkian wench. The truck view, from the rolled down monitors only, showed the truck reeling ever upward, ten, fifty, sixty nine feet high. Each stomach of each human inside felt the nervous pull of hovering and swaying from the autonomous helicopter.

The truck attached, dangled from the helicopter like a loose bag of po-tates in a child's grip, rushing toward the slowly flying, paragliding viper weasel and the sun shined cat in the box.

Krystal tugged on Nancy's tactical arm sleeve. "Why do they call it a viper weasel?"

Nancy's eyes flicked to and fro Brad for half a split second. "Well, they're Syns, synthetic-biological, computer controlled animals. And with that comes super speed, like a viper, intelligence, as long as the person on the other end is, which no doubt they usually are, and ability to use a variety of tools. Adding the second animal name, viper, also shows the weasel has gone through some varied biological changes and the high possibility it can kill. Haven't I already gone over this with you?"

The paraglider, box, truck and helicopter flew from city underneath to the freedom of the beautiful suburbs, gas stations and mini malls underfoot and undertruck, extra-large grocery stores for extra-large thinking citizens all around.

Nancy spoke to everyone and no one. "I swear, this is the longest and most ridiculous day I have ever had." She shook her head, looking to Brad, who was gripping the wheel, turning it with the turns of the helicopter above. "Brad?"

He was focused. "Huh." He didn't turn his head toward her, his eyes lay ahead, out of the open monitor.

"Are you pretending to control the helicopter from here?"

His fingers squeezed the wheel. He looked at her, letting go. He shook his head ever so quickly. "No, no. No, I wasn't trying to control the helicopter with my truck." Cough. "Anyway, we need some guns. I have a laser pulser in the bed, maybe you or Krystal could get it for me."

Nancy smacked Brad in the chest. "Stop trying to have a child handle the dang, frickin' guns! Jesus Heck Christ!" She pulled herself out of her seat, wiggling and wriggling back to the back for the second time against the slippery white patent leather.

Krystal's jaw dropped. "So that's his middle name."

Javon spoke over the truck speakers. "Nancy! You gotta stop saying that name. I'm getting something on radar, same sig as after you said it the first time."

Nancy pulled herself free of the confines of the truck, the air was cleaner, thinner, colder and faster as she stood low in the truck bed of the towed beast. Above, the helicopter chopped the air furiously, her feet rustling against the multitude of firearms riddling the truck bed. She grabbed a sniper rifle and the laser pulser as Brad suggested, slowly and carefully putting them into the cabin of the truck.

All of a sudden, blasts down below, on the ground of Earth 1.0, the original, blasted with explosion. And again. And again.

"Mortar blasts! What's going on?" She bellowed, her face in the cabin window. Brad grabbed the laser pulser, flipping the tiny monitor of the weapon ON. He shoved the barrel of the laser pulser out of the open monitor of his truck, Nancy did the same with the sniper rifle outside, resting it on the wall of the bed. She peered over the side, watching from nearly twelve thousand inches as a war tore through the boundary between Suburbia and the first orchards of the Agricultural zone.

She pressed her comm, speaking to Brad as the winds and war sounds were too loud to be overheard even from right outside. "I think the Latter Day Arborists are at it again. But who are they fighting?"

Javon's extra loud voice came over the truck speakers and Nancy's comm. "Well, a couple things are happening down there, girl. Look, you gotta stop sayin' homeboy's name in vain. He keeps popping up all over the place. Second, the Librariitians have called for the death of the New Arborists' leader, and then when Brad! Said a war on Jesus, well, Muhammad came down to Fatwah that cute lil' bootie. So we got a holy war and a war of books versus trees. It's a rager down there."

Nancy shook her head. "Why are the NAs fighting the Library System?"

Javon elaborated the complex socio-political system of the day. "They want all books to be composted, even the ones already in the System. Said it's their religion that all information must be forgotten. And they're offended if everyone else doesn't comply. This war will be over in a few weeks when they forget what they're fighting about. The thing to worry about is Muhammad and Jesus. Them two gonna get wil' n out."

Brad popped his head out of the back window, an LED moment. "Nancy! I know exactly how to get rid of Jesus and Muhammad!"

"How? We don't even know what Muhammad looks like, do we?"

Muhammad has the face like A LOT of other people—a nose, two ears, lips, a few or more tooths, black hair, eyeballs.

Brad shook his head. "It's time we stop pretending we don't know what Muhammad looks like. We know Jesus is a dark Arab guy with long hair and never had a girlfriend. Same with Muhammad. But I know the secret! Really, I do!"

Nancy grimaced, waiting to hear the worst.

"Pigs!" Brad yelled. "We call the pigs on them all. Jesus is, was a Jew. Muhammad is or was Muslim, apparently. Neither eats pork. Send a few fat boy hogs over there, round up some super pigs from the South and they'll run 'em out of town. Who needs em anyways?"

"Amen." Nancy said.

Javon spoke to them both. "Ya'll offensive."

"Oh really?" Nancy said.

Javon replied. "Yes."

"Well, deal with it. You heard the man. Call the pigs in, take care of this holy moly mess. In the meantime, we need to save this cat!"

Javon mumbled. "I forgot about the cat. Forty, over 'n out."

Nancy watched as Brad had his laser pulser pointed at the paraglider, the monitor showing a zoomed in image, the viper weasel turning the craft to the right, beyond, green grass and a crowd of people. Nancy hollered at him. "Brad! You know you can't shoot, right?"

He turned back to her. "Why? Should I aim left?"

She pointed. "There's people behind. You need a clear shot!"

"Oh!" He gruffed.

Nancy went on. "You know, we're in our own country. If these were civilians of another country, I'd say go for it, you know, that's what war is. But we can't have friendly fire here."

Brad agreed. "Yeah, yeah. All these stupid rules. I'll wait."

"Protecting the homeland means keeping everyone in it alive and healthy."

Brad shrugged. "Fine. Although, you're sounding a lot like communist Jesus right now, and I don't appreciate it. I'm about to be offended."

And as soon as the paragliding weasel fell free from the crowd below and in front of the line of sight of Brad's weapon, as soon as trees were the only thing possible to accidentally shoot if Brad missed, or the laser went through the weasel and out to burn into the ground three meters deep, which would definitely be the case, which is a little over three yards, Brad pulled the trigger. No recoil at all as Brad's finger triggered the trigger and the laser pulse dashed and zipped and zapped out of the barrel of the gun. The pulse shot through the air in an electric pink bolt, nearly arcing. A gust of wind and pressure dropped the paraglider, sending the cat in the box, on a cable, up. Brad saw the cat's eye glow yellow, grow as large as Muhammad's face as the laser pulse came for it. In an instant, a burst of rainbow light showered the sky as a universe came through the atmosphere. Pulsars and galaxies, blackholes and supernovae exploded in colour, stretching across time-space.

Krystal screamed. "Dingy! Dingy! Nooooo!"

The explosion shot through the atmosphere in all directions as the laser blasted into the microcosm which had been hanging off the cat's neck. Everyone in the truck knew what had happened. The microcosm destroyed, the cat was surely toast on sliced bread, nor could the weasel be alive. The paraglider was absent from space, from sky, from all. The universal explosion shone brightly, sticking to their retinas in afterglow as the helicopter and truck moved forward, toward the site in the air, Air Zero, wait, Air One, because zero doesn't count.

Krystal cried, Nancy pulled herself back into the cabin to care for the girl, to hug her as the tears flowed. A loud ding smacked from above, they all looked up, out of the rolled down monitors, trying to catch a glimpse.

METALLIC CRASH!

The bed of rifles was pummelled with a titanium box, dinging, bending, snapping guns left and right, top and bottom. Nancy shook, her voice not there. "Ohhh!" Slowly, she pulled herself through the cabin into the bed once again. Krystal alert, serious, wiping the tears away from her cheeks as she watched.

Nancy grabbed the metal box, jagged, serrated teeth, holes for air and slipping into like the trap it is. Carefully she picked it up to eye level, knowing how light the box was, there was no way a living cat was inside. Her stomach churned, hands quivered. Her eyes focused on something, fur, a yellow eye, a collar. Yes! It was a cat. She put a finger inside, shuffling just enough to move the cat closer to the edge of the box. The cat slid toward her, to the edge of the box. The cat's face pressed against the jagged toothed hole, unmoving, but upright. Nancy's stomach sank, her heart shrivelled, ran cold, confused. She short circuited. She looked to Krystal, fuming, dropping the box onto the floor of guns.

"The cat isn't real?!" Nancy had seen a hyper-realistic cat stuffed-toy. If from the 1990s, the greatest age of all time, one would call it a cat beanie baby.

Krystal shook her head. "I never said Dingy was alive."

Nancy stood up, erect, bellowing a whooping cry into the sky.

The weasel slid down the helicopter's cable as she did, jumping into the truck bed, grabbing the box, pirouetting off and into the sky below.

Nancy looked down once again, realising seconds later the box was gone. "What just happened?"

Brad replied. "The weasel grabbed the box as you were screaming. You couldn't here me."

"It's 'hear', not 'here'!" She climbed into the truck from the back window. "Let's just go home. This has been a complete waste of time." Nancy looked at Brad, biting his lip, nodding, understanding nothing.

Javon came over the truck speakers. "We apprehended the weasel, no thanks to you too."

Nancy roared. "Javon!" She started laughing, and laughing, becoming uncontrollable in her fit of delirium.

Brad looked at her. "Well, heck, what are the chances the cat was never alive?"

Space Hooray

Robin Drown

Dear Diary,

You'll be pleased to hear that I have finalised my list of the 'Worst Things about Being Stranded in Space'. Here it is:

1. No access to saved games on home PC.

2. Having to share a bathroom.

3. Frankie's aftershave.

4. No family, friends etc.

5.No Feasts or Twisters in the freezer.

Now, faithful Diary, I know I promised not to conform to any typical, cliché list sizes. We talked about how trite those 'top five' and 'top ten' lists can be, and what an absolute coincidence it is that there were exactly ten shocking moments in kids' TV shows that you didn't understand until you were a grown-up. The thing you have to understand is that Frankie smells really, really bad.

I don't know how he managed it. We had approximately thirty-five minutes to board the ship and get it into orbit before the feds cottoned on to us, and somehow, he managed to smuggle onboard enough of the stuff to keep him going for at least five months. He shows no signs of stopping, too. How much is left in that little bottle of his? The idea of being lost in the stars alongside Frankie's stinky neck and wrists for the next fifty years makes it hard to sleep at night. Or whenever it is we sleep.

Maybe Tony ("The Twat") gave Frankie extra warning, told him to fill his pockets with discounted eau de toilette way in advance. It would be just like him to tell Frankie and Happy and not tell me. If I had known, I would have loaded my Sonic the Hedgehog saves to the cloud.

While I'm complaining about my crewmates, I must make sure I add SARA to the list. She woke me up first thing this morning to complain about the G-Matrix.

"Gravity Matrix faulty; requires emergency repairs." she said. She reminded me of my mum.

I fondled around the table next to my bunk to find my alarm clock. "Jesus, SARA, it's not even ten o'clock."

"Crewmate M is required on the bridge to report to the Captain."

I rolled onto my side. "He's not the captain, he's a twat."

"Noted."

"No, don't... SARA, can I at least have some breakfast first?"

"Breakfast menu is not available." If I thought she was capable of it, I swear I heard some disdain in one of her beeps. I couldn't blame her though. We had danced the breakfast menu tango too many times over the last few months, and it wasn't her fault that the chef-bots were programmed to look at the clock. I had told Tony that maybe next time he decided to steal a military-grade spacecraft, he should check the onboard menus first.

I ordered something from the lunch menu, telling myself I could squint and pretend it was a brunch. I rolled out of bed and staggered down the corridor, yawning loudly and dramatically enough for anyone nearby to hear.

There was a loud, elongated beeping noise from one of the consoles that reminded me of dying in Donkey Kong or something. The G-Matrix had failed, because apparently I have to fix everything around here. I think I got some weird inverted whiplash from being shot up to the ceiling, shoulders-first. Nobody came to help me out so I was left hanging there like a marionette with terrible posture. Eventually, SARA rolled underneath me.

"Your sandwich, Crewmate M," she said.

"Fat lot of good that does me up here!" I replied, my chin tucked deeply into my neck fat. "Can you throw sandwiches, SARA?"

That was unfair and I apologised. SARA had not been built with arms. She was no SARA+++.

"Please can you tell Tony the... Captain... to fix the gravity and get me down from here!"

It wasn't SARA's fault but I shouted at her regardless. She's an emotionless husk but I still feel a little bad when I yell or throw shoes at her. She beeped, placed the sandwich directly below me on the smooth metal floor of the corridor, and wheeled herself off to the bridge.

I looked down longingly at the sandwich and thought of Donkey Kong.

I must have been up there for at least twenty minutes. My stomach growled three times. I could smell something burning coming from the direction of the engine room. Knowing this lot, they were probably having a barbeque without me.

Eventually, the G-Matrix kicked back in and I dropped down to the floor. It hurt every single part of my body apart from the small patch on my right thigh that landed in the ham and cheese sandwich. I was now bruised all over and stunk of butter and cheddar. I sounded like the start of a joke.

"Are you alright?" Tony was standing over me, looking down on my bruised but delicious body. I bet he loved lording it up over me like that. Like a big ol' Zeus.

"Yes," I lied. "What happened to the G-Matrix?"

"It failed at six o'clock this morning. Weren't you supposed to be on maintenance duty today?"

The tone in his voice told me everything I needed to know. The fancy-pants fake captain wanted to blame this on me. But this was my carnival, and I wouldn't let him knock this coconut off the coconut-thing and win a fluffy teddy bear.

"Sorry," I said, as insincerely as I could. "I was up late last night."

"What were you doing?"

"Writing." I spoke too quickly, and bit my lip.

He asked me what I had been writing. Just a side note here, Diary – I am afraid to say I have been cheating on you. I have a mistress. She is a gorgeous A4 pad that I use for poetry. I had spent the night on a bit of a poetry-bender after my debut recital with SARA had resulted in some mild crushing disappointment. After I finished reading each poem to her and asked for her opinion, she would say something like 'I can confirm that was a poem' or 'I have completed listening to the poem.' It's all well and good having AI that can cook your meals and organise your days and restart your heart, but what's stopping them from giving you an ego boost once in a while?

I didn't want to tell Tony that I was up until 4 o'clock trying to write some verses that would impress a robot, so I lied.

"I was writing home. You know. I know they'll never read it or anything but it makes me feel better..."

Tony nodded. His cheeks flushed slightly. He had fallen for it, hook, line, and sinker. Good ol' guilt, always gets you out of a jam.

"Well..." he said. It was practically an apology. "Next time, just let somebody know if you don't think you'll make your shift. We're a team, right?"

"Right." He extended his hand and pulled me back to my feet. He nodded, patted a stray crust from my stained thigh, and held me for a moment by the shoulders before smiling broadly and returning to the bridge. What a prick.

"SARA, get me another sandwich. I'll be in my room."

I rubbed my sore arm, yawned, and went back to bed, having achieved exactly nothing since waking up. You see why I called this journal 'Space Hooray', right? This is the worst fun I've ever had.

***

It has been five days since the sandwich-and-gravity incident. My sincerest apologies, my dearest Diary! I did not intend to neglect you. Unfortunately I have been locked in some sort of Bio-Cell since Tuesday, and no matter how many times I complained, I had no access to my diary, fresh water, First Aid or my Sega Game Gear.

It started shortly after I had finished my ham and cheese sandwich. Sensing my foul mood, SARA had kindly instructed the chef-bots to make it with extra ham and extra cheese. I didn't say anything, and she didn't say anything either, but I knew what she had done, and I was grateful. It was a great sandwich and I would have said something to SARA about it but we were called to the bridge (for the second time in two hours!) for yet another 'emergency.'

"Something's beeping the left wall!" Tony explained. I was making a big show of dragging myself into the bridge and yawning, but none of them could be bothered with paying me any attention. Don't mind me, then.

Given that none of us are trained astronauts or space-mans, we had to improvise a lot of the terminology we use on the ship. 'The left wall' was where the radar and navigation systems sat. If it was 'humming', 'tweeping', 'twooping', 'scratching' or 'moo-eep-ing', it was doing something it was supposed to be doing, so we left it alone. But it had never 'beeped' before. The flight console was the thing that was supposed to be doing the beeping.

Frankie suggested pressing the blue button on the left wall that was now flashing in time with the beeps. I could barely hear him over the sound of his cologne.

Without even checking with me, Tony leaned forward and pressed it gingerly. We waited for what seemed like ten seconds but was actually more like six.

"—immediate boarding. Repeat: This is Earth Zone Military Police Unit #14. This is a signal for the acting crew onboard the stolen military vehicle Blair IV. We are requesting permission for-"

Tony cut them off. "What do we do?" He was practically drowning in sweat. Some captain he was, looking to his crew for advice.

"Well, we don't let them on," I said. They ignored me.

"Can we just ignore them and speed off, like?" Happy was breathless, as if the act of thinking and then speaking was too much for him.

"I imagine they've got missiles." Tony nervously covered his mouth, making it even harder to hear his already shaky voice. Some leader!

"Do we have missiles?" Frankie asked.

"I'm not getting into a fire-fight with the army," Tony said, waving his hand dismissively. Just goes to show what he really thinks of his crew, doesn't it?

"I've got an idea. M, open comms!" Happy was practically barking at me.

"You're not in charge!" I responded, but then I realised that I was the one standing closest to the 'Open Communications' button.

Tony looked confused but not entirely unrelieved. Happy leaned in closer to Tony in order to whisper his plan, which I assume was just to make sure I didn't hear about it. I did hear though, so joke's on him.

"These ships are piloted by AI. Maybe we can confuse it."

"How? By asking it to draw some hands?" Tony replied. Okay, even I had to admit that was a good one.

Happy shook off the joke and spoke into the microphone. "This is the crew of the Blair IV. Requesting reason for boarding."

The response came through instantly. Well, near enough. "You have stolen the Blair IV. We have the warrants for your arrest. Comply and you will be treated with something resembling mercy."

Happy pondered over his response for a little too long. I almost jumped in to save the day. He pressed the button before I decided to take action.

"I'm afraid you've got the wrong ship," He said. "This here is a cargo ship... for orphans. I mean, toys for orphans. We're not orphans."

"I am," Frankie decided to add.

"Incorrect." The voice was mechanical in the way SARA's was, but it sounded a little more human, which in this case, was a very bad thing. "Anthony Dawes. Theodore Dawes. Frank Dudley. Gareth Green. Mason Marks. You are all under arrest."

Why was I last on that list? Even the AI doesn't respect me.

None of my so-called 'more competent' crewmates said anything, so I stepped up to the plate, as the Americans say, and scored a slam-dunk.

"Negative, Unit #14. Scan for life forms on our ship. There are only four of us." I released the button and squeezed out from the space I had made between Tony and Lucky's shoulders. They looked at me with facial expressions that I had only ever seen on begging dogs.

"Inconclusive, Blair IV. That proves absolutely nothing."

I sighed and quietly made my way to the back of the room.

***

Needless to say, the police AI boarded and captured us in Bio-Cells that they strapped against the walls of the bridge of our stolen Navy ship. I had never seen one used in real life before. They don't look like they look on the TV. They look more... I don't know... budget. There's still a neon web of part-organic wire-chain that holds you in place, but the colours look less vibrant than you would expect. The living prison that they tied me up in was red, but it was the most phoned-in red I had ever laid eyes on.

They even locked SARA up in one, although due to her lacking any organic matter, they kept her in place with a giant magnet. I thought it was hardly fair to lump SARA in with the rest of us – she hadn't knowingly done anything wrong, she was just doing what she was told. Still, if generations of people before me hadn't stood up against police brutality, I wasn't about to start.

The military police AI resembled SARA in the way the human version of the Terminator resembled the robo-skeleton death machine version of the Terminator. Where SARA had all of her internal systems covered in polished pastel panels and a smiling face terminal screen, the computer-y bits that made up this AI were covered only in bullet-proof glass. Underneath the glass, you could see his glowing blue orb brain flicker and spasm, looking like a Tesla coil recovering from a hostile divorce. Their tank tracks were practically the same, although the police AI had a dorky name badge attached to the front, declaring that his name was 'Officer NATHAN'.

NATHAN paced up and down in front of us. I say 'paced', but the AI units were hardly known for their speed. I guess it would be accurate to say that he was 'moving'. You couldn't deny that he was getting from one place to another... eventually.

He looked me up and down. "Where is the human designated Theodore Dawes?"

Tony interrupted and answered the question that was obviously meant for me.

"He's up your arse!" Tony declared. This was ridiculous because AI don't have arses, and if they did, I'm sure NATHAN would have noticed having a six foot tall man up there.

If NATHAN had a face like SARA, he probably would have rolled his eyes. As it is, he just did an angry beep and his blue lights dulled gently for a nano-second. NATHAN turned to face SARA.

"Elaborate," NATHAN instructed his mechanical sister.

"No crew or guest registered as 'Theodore Dawes'." SARA replied.

"He didn't make it on with the rest of us..." Tony grumbled, giving away more than he should have, if you ask me. "He made the ultimate sacrifice to ensure society wouldn't be overrun by tyrannical AI tanks like you!"

"Spoken like a true criminal," NATHAN said. It's true I don't know too many criminals so I can't exactly corroborate but I'm pretty sure that's not accurate.

"It is of little consequence. Anthony Dawes. Frank (he said all the names. I'm not listing them all again. If you liked it so much, just go back a couple of pages and read it again). You are all under arrest for the theft of a military vehicle, breaking and entering into military and private property, resisting arrest, and other crimes. You may pay £4.19 to have these crimes listed and emailed directly to you. You will need a Military Police Online Account in order to..."

NATHAN read us the rest of the terms and conditions of our crimes, and then read us our rights. As we listened, I swore I heard Frankie starting to cry. Thinking about it now though, it might have just been the faulty ventilation piping that I was supposed to have fixed.

"You will now be escorted back to Earth to stand trial."

"Query." SARA said, her voice firmer and louder than I had ever heard it. Me and the other humans strapped to the wall held our breath. My heart skipped a beat. Had she just...

NATHAN rotated in order to face her. A system of hydraulics and levers in his chassis lifted the jar that contained his brain orb up and right into SARA's perpetually grinning face screen. With his voice in 'gritted teeth' mode, he said "Explain."

"Holding human suspects in Bio-Cells qualifies as 'cruel and unusual punishment' as defined by the Geneva Convention 2." SARA sounded like the one teacher who actually managed to spot the bullies picking on you.

"Denied. They present a risk to others and, most relevantly, me."

"Agreed." SARA said politely. Her onscreen avatar blinked. "But you are obligated to provide sufficient entertainment during the journey back to Earth."

NATHAN fell silent for a moment. His blue lights flashed to the left and then to the right. Eventually, he said "Agreed. What will be considered adequate entertainment, Hospitality Unit SARA?"

Ouch. Rude.

I was going to suggest my Sega Game Gear, but SARA did not miss a beat.

"Poetry."

The other three gasped loudly. Perhaps they had cottoned on to the plan as quickly as I had. I could not see the expressions on their faces but I was sure they were flushed with excitement.

"Poetry?" NATHAN sounded genuinely curious.

"Regular poetry readings are often performed by Crewmate Mason Marks. They are very popular among the crew."

"Uh..." I heard Frankie and Tony say in unison. Lucky might have said something too but his stomach made a gurgling noise that would have drowned it out.

"Query!" NATHAN barked. "It is not..."

SARA ignored him. "Crewmate M, please could you assist Officer NATHAN and conduct a reading."

I cleared my throat. This was my moment to shine. Now, Diary, I swore to myself in the mirror years ago that I would never cross fiction with non-fiction, never mix my art with my memoirs. However, I feel I cannot tell this story with its intended dramatic weight if I do not print the poems I delivered here in your pages.

As I said, I cleared my throat, and I poemed.

Island, island, sea and sun

Island, island, tropical fun

I wish I could be

Swimming in your sea

But I am swimming in space

Unwillingly

Now, the response I got from the assembled humans and robots was not the reaction I had fantasised about getting after my first public performance, but it was technically a reaction.

"I can confirm that I have listened to a poem," SARA said. I had heard those words many times, but only from SARA. It came as a shock to hear them also come from NATHAN.

Not that much of a shock though because I knew what SARA's plan was at this point. Forget I said anything about it being a shock.

"...Now, I must..." NATHAN tried to speak.

"Another poem, please, Crewmate M."

I delivered one on a silver platter with a side of curly fries and onion rings. I was also hungry.

I like music

I like rap

I like Shaggy and N-Trance

I like reggae

I like funk

I like to tear the dance floor up

"I can confirm that was a poem," SARA said.

"...was a poem," echoed NATHAN. "I must return to..."

I fired another one out of the six-shooter.

I was walking down the street one day

And I said to my mate

I said "Hey, you, what you doing?"

He said "I'm starting a revolution"

"Oh God..." Frankie groaned. "This is like Hitch-Hikers' Guide to the Galaxy, but it's shit!"

Obviously he was too slow on the uptake to realise what the plan was. Of course it's obvious to me and you, right, Diary? That's why I'm not bothering to explain it.

"Poem has been received." NATHAN spoke again in his even-more-robotic voice, then switched back to his normal still-quite-robotic tone. "I must now return to my craft for charging..."

"I've not got nothing to say here," I announced proudly and loudly. "I've got not something to play here…"

"Ugh!" Happy decided to add. Perhaps he thought of himself as some sort of hype-man.

"I have completed listening to a poem." NATHAN said when I was finished. "Battery level is currently 54% and…"

"La-de-dah, rainbows are lovely…"

"I can confirm that was a poem." SARA said when that one was done. "Please read another, Crewmate M…"

NATHAN beeped loudly. "Battery level currently at 53% and…"

***

His battery was fully drained around about the fifteenth reading of 'Island'. My crewmates, I must add, did not offer to help at all at any point, even when I offered them a duet. Frankie fell asleep after about two hours. I think Lucky did too, or he fainted, one or the other. He vomited on himself beforehand though. Tony managed to stay awake, but he still felt the need to pray quite audibly.

I looked at the still and deflated tank-robot-man that had been trying desperately to crawl towards the exit in-between poems. I was going to spit on him but I had no idea what kind of reach I had.

"How come your battery didn't drain too, SARA?" Tony asked. Not a terrible question.

"I can wirelessly charge from the ship's engine..." The GIF that was her face turned towards me. "...in situations like this one."

"How long have we got until the Bio-Cells run out of juice?" I asked. It was a subjectively better question.

"Approximately a week."

I must admit that it was my turn to faint.

***

Frankie and Happy pushed the brick that was once Officer NATHAN into the rear of the ship. I was going to offer to help but it really looked like more of a two-person job. Instead, I had been tasked with keeping watch on the radar. Tony seemed to be convinced that this was a very, very important job that only someone with my skill set could do, but I wondered what the big deal was.

Tony asked SARA if she had patched through to the control system of the now-abandoned military police ship, to which she beeped in the positive. All we needed to do now was spacewalk over there and take off our shoes. With a little manual labour – which I was more than happy to leave to the others, given the ordeal I had just gone through – we would be able to wire SARA in to replace NATHAN as the onboard AI and we would have a ship that was inferior to our current ship in every way.

Wait, that sounds bad. Yes, the ship we stole was vastly superior to the police ship, but it had been run down by five months of a bunch of amateurs (and me, I can't deny I may have made a few mistakes somewhere down the line) and it was, as they say in those movies where cool people steal cars, 'hot'.

"Who would've thought..." Tony said. His voice was light and annoyingly comforting but he was speaking loudly enough so the whole crew could hear. "...That AI's inability to truly escape human control was..."

"I think we've all learned a lesson today!" I stepped in with a louder and firmer voice. Tony looked at me as if I had just descended from the heavens and landed in his bowl of cereal. "AI will always be too dependent on us humans to present any real threat! It was because of my... our ingenuity to force that thing to drain its battery that we survived! We used its weaknesses to defeat it – using the very human properties of ingenuity, resourcefulness and, yes, dare, I say, art!"

It was quite a rousing speech. Everybody looked as if they had never heard anything like it before. They all turned to SARA, who had animated an awkward expression on her monitor face.

"...Yeah." That was all Tony was able to say.

Confident that I had finally made my mark, maybe earned a little respect around here, I turned to SARA myself and smiled widely.

"Now, SARA, how about a sandwich?"

The answer to the fermi paradox

Aaron Frale

"Paperclips," Gleeglub said. His name wasn't really Gleeglub, nor did he actually say anything. His real name included tones and sounds unpronounceable by human anatomy. He also doesn't convey sonic information via vocal cords, so it's not quite speech. However, this story is written in English, and Gleeglub saying, "Paperclips" is the best we can do.

Even using the pronouns of he/him is a pale representation of the actual gender of Gleeglub, who is more of a shez on the gender spectrum. In fact, "paperclip" isn't even accurate because what most humans would recognize as a paperclip actually resembles the reproductive organ of one of the forty-two genders of his species. Even "species" doesn't quite describe the beings to which Gleeglub belongs because it's more of a hive or matrix, and even those words explain only about 13.5% of the concept of categorization for beings like Gleeglub.

We could continue to nitpick the inadequacies of using English to describe the moment of space time where Gleeglub said, "Paperclips", but then we'd never complete the story. So, let it suffice as:

"Paperclips."

"What?" Bob responded. Bob was his real name and actually sounds like Bob in English. His consortium of parents were fans of the Earth comedian, Bob Hope.

"Paperclips," Gleeglub repeated. "The entire planet is covered in paperclips. There is nothing left – no humans, no plants, no animals, not even the paperclip factory."

"What do you suppose happened?" Bob said.

"We could roll back the recording, but in this case, I think it's safe to assume that they created an AI to make paperclips."

"They didn't program ethics?"

"Ethics eats into the bottom line," Gleeglub joked. Once again, it wasn't really a joke. More of a complex statement of morality and irony that most of his species learn when they are infants.

Not that "infant" accurately describes the gestation period, which happens partially outside the womb. But we digress.

"Move on to the next galaxy?" Bob asked.

"'Fraid so..." Gleeglub replied, and a moment later, they were at another identical replica of planet Earth around the star Sol. Exactly how they got there and what they were traveling inside is too complicated to describe in English, but when a species has had the entirety of the universe's existence minus several million years to evolve and innovate, they've had time to create some almost mystical-seeming technology.

For example, they'd created an exact copy of the Solar system in every galaxy in the universe based on Earth circa November 16, 1974 when the Arecibo radio telescope sent the intentional signal into space attempting to contact what was out there. Gleeglub's species took the signal as affirmation that Earth was ready to join the universe, and therefore would have no problem with aliens who'd advanced for 13 billion or so years doing whatever they wanted with the planet.

Gleeglub had every intention of answering the age-old question of why his was the only advanced species in the entire universe. In the 13 billion or so years that his people had wandered the stars, every single intelligent species had annihilated itself before they could get off their planet and explore their galaxy. The paperclip moment for every species except Gleeglub's was called the Great Filter. He figured that now, with as many Earths as there were galaxies, if even one survived the Great Filter, he could figure out what made his own species so special.

Yes, the star charts and all historical references to them were changed with each iteration to fit the new galaxy. And no, we won't explain! Because we can't. Imagine trying to explain to a dragonfly how your Subaru works. Sure, in 3.7% of the Earths where humans had already annihilated themselves, dragonflies evolved to be the next dominant intelligent species of the planet, but that doesn't mean a dragonfly circa 1974 would have the slightest clue about combustion and pistons. Don't get caught up in the details!

Anyway, humans were perfect for the experiment because they were versatile, as pregalactic species go. For example, if a species was too warlike, they'd off themselves the moment they discovered nuclear weapons. If they were too passive, television would do them in. Some would melt their planet with nanomachines. Others would ignore asteroids, while some would worship them and redirect them toward their home planet. There was even a species of hyperintelligent plants that did themselves in with hydroponic farming.

The point was that humans seemed to be a little bit of everything – sometimes they'd destroy their civilization with nuclear war, and others involved bananas. If one of the experiments was heading down a path too similar to an iteration that had already happened, Gleeglub would nudge the civilization by making a billionaire buy Twitter, or creating an unstoppable boy band, to vary the results. Don't get too caught up on how he does this. His species has had 13 billion or so years to refine. Humans are lucky if they make it for a couple hundred from when the entire planet begins at November 16, 1974 all over again.

Despite the tweaks, and the countless iterations of Earth throughout the universe, the humans found creative new ways to do themselves in. For example, the climate crisis that was already in progress when the Earth was replicated and dumped into other galaxies spawned all manner of apocalyptic events. From the version that ignored the problem and ended up like Venus, to the one that decided the way to fix the climate crisis involved filling the Earth's oceans with cheese.

That one we can explain. Since the holes in Swiss cheese are created via bacteria farts containing carbon dioxide, and the ocean also helps cycle carbon out of the air, it was postulated that perhaps cheese in the ocean would keep it there. It became apocalyptic when a fast food chain created the ocean Swiss and mushroom patty melt and Brad Pitt did the commercial.

Climate change alone had destroyed humanity on 85,789,350,234 iterations. They ignored it, exasperated it, and all manner of either hiding from the problem or causing more problems with unintended consequences. For example, one solution was glitter in the atmosphere to reflect sunlight. While the sparkles corrected the problem, they had created super boy bands with glittery skin, and it's a documented fact that boy bands are a harbinger of the apocalypse. It seemed that humans would much rather imagine the gentle caress of their favourite hunky singer than innovate ways to survive the Great Filter.

Because of the law of unintended consequences (it's a simple law – there'll be consequences, deal with it), AI has repeatedly created a tricky hurdle for humanity. In one iteration, a researcher created a chatbot with the goal of destroying humanity. They turned it off after a few laughs, and failed to realize it created copies of itself, and those copies achieved the goal by creating the most powerful force in recruiting followers, a boy band. The Earth was doomed in songs of teen hormones and weapons of mass destruction.

Another version had created AI to save humanity, armed with the collective knowledge about the power of savings. It converted the humans into paper money, opened a high interest savings account, and put the dollars made from the carbon atoms of humans into the account. This particular Earth is now the wealthiest of all the failed Earths, due to compound interest. However, there are no humans left to enjoy the wealth.

Then there was the AI that was programmed to make Jenkins happy, and Jenkins was most happy when he was alone, so it killed all the humans. Technically, Jenkins survived the Great Filter, but Gleeglub wasn't sure that counted. There were AI versions that tore apart an entire galaxy to make Taylor Swift's new album, boiled the oceans to fulfill a prank order for 5 billion crab legs, destroyed the Sun so we could get some sleep, genetically modified every male to look like Brad Pitt, split the Earth in half to "get a look at those reptile people", and even blew up the planet for "a really sweet action movie sequence".

It seemed that the more times humans attempted to create AI, the more they botched it up by not examining the consequences for the future. Perhaps the Great Filter was simply that humans didn't have good long-term thinking skills. Maybe evolved intelligence by its very definition was short term in nature.

For example, perhaps when the first of Gleeglub's species foraged for berries (for his kind, berries are more of a quasi-dimensional convergence rather than a fruit), intelligence was an asset that helped his ancestors gather more food. Then when farming, and as a byproduct, societies emerged, those with short-term goals were the most successful, and long-term thinkers were weeded out of the gene pool, which would then cause the intelligence to act in terms of immediate gains over long-term survival.

Thus the Great Filter of long-term planning and thinking, having no immediate advantage over short-term, is bred out. And by the time the species needs long-termness to survive, it's already gone from the gene pool.

But this explanation was a little too simple, so Gleeglub didn't believe it. There were examples of human civilization acting with long-term thinking. There were architecture projects that took generations to finish, thus ensuring the originators would be dead before it was finished. People buried Cheetos in ten-thousand-year tombs for future generations to access. Nuclear waste dumps were given stone and metal tablets to warn about the dangers to future generations. In every iteration, Voyager I was launched with a slightly different golden record, meant to be played by some civilization of the distant future. Gleeglub's favorite was one with another cheese ocean, inviting the galaxy to come to Taco Tuesday on planet Earth.

In every iteration, there was somebody who wanted to build a civilization like Star Trek, that worked for the betterment of humanity. One iteration even succeeded in creating the United Federation of Planets with its headquarters in San Francisco, USA. That particular iteration died from plastic Vulcan ears poisoning.

"Another dead one," Bob commented.

The Earth below them was very much a lifeless world. The biomass had been slopped together to look like a giant Earth-sized anus so the planet could moon the moon. Gleeglub couldn't even begin to imagine what had happened, but assumed it was AI, and filed it away.

"On to the next one," Bob said.

Gleeglub was now depressed. Once again, it's not quite what humans know as depression, but more a complicated mixture of chemical and electrical impulses, a trans-dimensional time clock, and an urge to pee. He wasn't sure if he'd ever find the answer. The universe was 13 billion or so years old. He figured that at least one species in some star system should have managed to leave their planetary home and join the intergalactic community. But so far, nothing. Just lots of Earths, and lots of disaster.

He had decided to end his own existence because he wasn't sure there would ever be an answer. His people were unique. He bought life-halting medicines from the local suicide clinic, threw a raging end-of-life party, and spent one last day with each of his 37 million children, all before Bob knew he was gone. Please, we can't explain – it's like explaining why Black Holes transmogrify matter in conjunction with parallel universes with different fundamental laws of physics, such as a giggle instead of Planck's constant, or what it feels like to get a neutron star massage. We just can't give the topic the complexity it deserves.

"Where'd you go?" Bob asked.

"To kill myself," Gleeglub said.

"Oh, that sucks. Should I end the Earth experiment and obliterate all the others?" Bob said. This is exactly as it sounds. Bob had a button that would wipe all traces of humanity from existence.

"Wait! What's going on with that one?!" Gleeglub pointed out the window. IT'S NOT A WINDOW! AN APPROXIMATION OF A WINDOW.

At this point, it's safe to wonder why the authors are writing this story in English if most of the concepts are too complicated for a human mind to comprehend. If it's causing the authors that much anxiety that they feel the need to write in all caps, then perhaps that sounds like a personal problem and not a fault of the reader. We apologize for any inadequacy the human reader may feel based on the authors' unwillingness to entertain the idea that the human reader will get it.

Which is precisely why Gleeglub was shocked about what he saw out the window. Above an obviously thriving planet was a large sign, written in English – "Welcome, Aliens!" The humans wrote it in English rather than some of the more popular languages of the planet such as Spanish or Chinese because it was the stunt of an American billionaire. Zooming in on the message would reveal that each letter of "Welcome, Aliens!" and the exclamation point were comprised of tiny messages written by the people of this version of Earth.

With a ten-dollar entry fee to the contest, any human could leave whatever message they wanted, and all the messages would construct the words "Welcome, Aliens!" and be launched into space. The individuals wrote all manner of things, from "it will be super cool to meet you" to "You anal probe me and I'll end you", "give me back my dog", "get off my lawn", and "Pete's Burritos 2 for $1".

The winner of that contest was Zach Underwireman, not to be confused with comic book legend Underwearman. Zach U and a couple of other celebrities would get to travel first class in a "genuine spaceship" to "greet them aliens". However, the billionaire had no actual intention of sending anyone up to meet Gleeglub because the entire stunt was designed to fund his legal fees for a criminal case of 34 felony counts of falsifying business records. The billionaire had cleverly worded that Zach U and his celebrity companions would only get the voyage if aliens presented themselves to the planet Earth.

Gleeglub arrived in his spaceship and messed it all up. Once again, "spaceship" is used loosely. It's the equivalent of calling the measurement of the entirety of creation a lovely picture. The arrival screwed up the billionaire's plans to never fund an expedition to meet the aliens, which triggered a lawsuit by Zach U and his celebrity companions for the billionaire to "pony up" for the emissaries of Earth. About five years after Gleeglub's arrival, the humans sent a ship out to greet them aliens.

For Gleeglub, the five years were spent debating with Bob the ethics of meeting the Earthlings, and by the time they considered every possibility, they figured, "Why not? It was the humans that started all this with that bloody 1974 message."

Keep in mind two essential facts. One, since Gleeglub and Bob are from the single alien species that survived the Great Filter, they spend a lot of time deliberating all possibilities before acting so as not to inadvertently annihilate their species. For example, it took them a million years to decide to go through with their experiment, five hundred thousand to gain approvals, two hundred thousand to find the right species when, luckily enough, humans signaled they were ready for the experiment in 1974 – almost two million years after the night Gleeglub and Bob drank too much fermented fruit (ALCOHOL ONLY SLIGHTLY DESCRIBES IT. REMEMBER WHAT WE SAID ABOUT BERRIES!) and thought up the idea of replicating a planet near its own extinction.

The second fact is that Gleeglub and Bob only sound British because Dr. Who has the most depictions of aliens in a single series, and all the aliens sound British. Therefore, in order to fit the essence of their being into a construct that humans could understand, they settled on British accents and green lizard suits that were reminiscent of something from the original Star Trek series that William Shatner would have finished off with a double fist punch. This second fact becomes more important because the emissaries from Earth included the replica of William Shatner.

Keep in mind that anyone who was alive on planet Earth in 1974 had replicas of themselves in every single galaxy living divergent lives since November 16, 1974. For the purposes of limited human understanding, a replica is like a more robust clone. Think of a clone as the bread one would get from a stone milling tool and a fire pit, where a replica is more like the bread one would get from an omnipotent being using their cosmic Cuisinart to make a nice sourdough.

This was how Zach U, William Shatner, the pop artist TayTay, Tom Cruise, and tech journalist Z found themselves to be the very first humans ever to meet an alien species.

The day started with all the usual fanfare where the billionaire, despite having 34 felony convictions, gave a speech from his luxury prison accommodations about how this historic moment was all his idea, and ranting about how his political rivals had framed him all along. Afterwards, the two supermodels hired to host the live-streamed event offered their show of support for the billionaire and spent thirty minutes shaming the world for being so critical of a visionary.

Zach U's speech was cut short after saying "Hi", and William Shatner only had time to quote his famous line from the original series about boldly going places and giving a "live long and prosper" salute. The others were cut out of the opening ceremony because the billionaire's rant had gone over, and the rocket was ready to launch.

Along with Zach, the motley crew of celebrities was shoved into a rocket, launched into space, and vomited upon by the lucky winner who had never left Toledo before he got on a plane to Florida. He had assumed that all the vomit would have been gone from his system despite the fact that the plane ride was a full two days before the space flight.

The world's scientists were a little nervous about Zach being an emissary for humanity, as he showed no clear understanding of human biology and a shaky grasp of science, at best. When asked a question about evolution, he responded, "Isn't that butterflies or something?" For physics, he stated, "I made a volcano for my science fair project." And for chemistry, he said, "I'd like an ibuprofen, thank you."

Others thought Zach was exactly the person you'd want, because he kinda floated between jobs. He'd worked at call centres, gas stations, three different Goodwills, and most recently as a receptionist at a yoga studio. Most people called him your everyday person – a real person and not a packaged celebrity.

In fact, it was never more apparent what an everyday guy Zach was than by a mere perusal of his social media postings. Despite having a couple hundred thousand followers because of the fact that he was humanity's emissary, he mostly posted pictures of his breakfast, a smattering of dumb memes, and a few comments about whatever college team was playing. Despite being voted the world's most boring social media account for three years running, he still got sponsorships for being Earth's emissary.

Which was why when he vomited on his track suit and sneakers provided by his sponsor for the trip, there were immediate memes, GIFs, and general ridicule. When the President of the United States of America was asked why they hadn't sent any government officials, he shrugged it off and said that the billionaire was a personal friend of his and "knows what he is doing".

By the time the two ships docked with each other, the world was in a frenzy. Keep in mind that it wasn't so much a docking, but rather the Earth ship being enveloped in a cocoon of calming, warming light. The emotional fervour of people on Earth ranged from those excited to reach a new era of peace and prosperity for humankind to those who were gearing up for the apocalypse and firing up the generators of their bunkers.

Once the gravity simulators brought the crew gently to their cabin floor, their craft dissolved around them until the crew, including the two pilots, stood in a patch of white nothingness that was actually Gleeglub's lavatory. Once Zach's sick was cleaned from their clothes and hair via a method that resembled evaporation and felt slightly ticklish, they instantly seemed to appear in a lounge that, to Zach, resembled a Six Flags snack bar where he, at eight years old, had tasted the best cheesy pretzel he would ever eat in his life. To TayTay, it appeared as the McDonald's she was in when she got a call about a record contract. William Shatner's version was that place in Hollywood with the little umbrellas. Tom Cruise was in a hotel bar where he met his number one fan, and Z was in a steel smelting foundry.

With each of the humans put at ease by their happy place, Gleeglub and Bob decided to stroll in with their lizard suits, which were only about 4.3% of their corporeal form. The rest of their bodies were in other-dimensional planes inaccessible by human physics. Through hyper-variant sonic modulation quasiparticle technology, Gleeglub constrained his voice to a frequency and pitch the humans could understand and said, "Hello, humans!"

To which the collective Earth watching the live-streaming event with bated breath screamed in a paroxysm of relief as tensions, fears, elation, and other emotions rode like a shockwave through the collective consciousness of all the people waiting on the planet. Men, women, children, and nongendered binaries, cried tears of joy, relief and fright as humanity experienced something bigger than Apollo 11 or the coronation of any queen. They knew without a doubt that they were not alone in the universe.

The Fermi Paradox finally had an answer. Its answer was not that intelligent life was reckless, selfish, and always marching towards its own inevitable annihilation. There wasn't a super advanced AI with billions of years to adapt systematically destroying any life that could remotely pose a threat. There wasn't even a set of laws like the Prime Directive in Star Trek where advanced cultures are not allowed to contact ones in earlier stages of development, because there didn't need to be. Most humans do not seek anthills deep in the Sonoran Desert to discuss particle physics. Why would Gleeglub's species contact humans?

And that was the answer to the burning question of the Fermi Paradox. Techno signatures of Gleeglub's species were all around if humans knew where to look. Say humans invented a Spectrographic Quasi Info Neutrino Array Emitter Pulse Phasic Detection Nano Determinator and Espresso Maker, the latter being exactly as it sounds. Like all cultures that borrow from each other, Starbucks could be found everywhere one would find a member of Gleeglub's species. There were three on his spaceship alone.

Anyway, say humans harness the power of neutrinos to scan for quasi particles folded into sixty separate dimensions under pressure equivalent to a black hole with boson fluctuations during antiquark disturbances on a spacetime variant of axiom constants while enjoying a caramel macchiato, then perhaps they would notice the... Sorry, we got away from ourselves. Let's restart this thought. Let's say humans invented technology that could detect Gleeglub's species – they wouldn't have a Fermi Paradox.

Their "aloneness" in the cosmos was simply a factor of not knowing the right questions to ask. Suffice it to say that the answer to the Fermi Paradox is simply that humans don't know the right questions to ask to provide themselves with a satisfying answer. Thus, Gleeglub didn't either, perhaps there was a species out there who viewed his kind as an anthill in the Sonoran desert.

However, there was one human who knew the right question to ask. Zach U, for all his boring plainness despite being Earth's emissary, Zach U for each time he was voted having the world's most boring social media account, or crowned most unexciting human alive, or why do we continue to write articles about uninteresting Zach U when we are clearly bored with the content... Despite all that, Zach U asked the right question.

Deep within the tapestry that comprised the "Welcome, Aliens!" banner unfurled in orbit around Earth was Zach U's message to the aliens. In a single historic moment, he actually asked something that would change Gleeglub's and human history forever. He had written, "SUP?"

To which Gleeglub answered, "Not much."

Thus it was forever known that life happens, if one takes the time to experience it, and perhaps have a nice Café au lait while it's happening.

That is, until William Shatner was inspired by his social media to do the double fist punch on the lizard guy as a joke. Which wasn't humanity's best idea.

Sincerely,

-The Intergalactic Association of Confederated Races to Transcend the Great Filter and Baristas Union.

Meet the authors

Meet Aaron Frale

This whimsical being screams and plays heavy metal guitar in the indie prog band, Spiral, and sometimes writes humorous fantasy novels. He is the author of Time Burrito, which for reasons outside the editor's understanding, is always free for everyone. Here's a synopsis.

With great burrito comes great responsibility. Pete's food truck at the University of New Mexico isn't going well. Seniors dare freshman to eat his burritos. Frats use them for pledges and pranks. Rumours fly around campus that they are chupacabra ground up with rat. Pete needs a change, and it comes in the form of a physics experiment gone awry. After being sucked into the past, he stumbles across an ingredient that goes great in one of his creations. First, there was Marty McFly. Then there was Bill and Ted. And now Pete...

Praise for Time Burrito

★★★★★

"Time Burrito is a fun read. My favourite characters were Misako and Unk. Unk is a merry prankster . . . his antics will make you laugh."

Meet John Coon

John Coon promises he isn't a holographic robot clone of a ghost sent from the future to conquer the galaxy. He is in fact one part sports journalist and one part science fiction and horror author blended together in a mad science experiment to see how many words one human can write before their hands fall off at the wrists. John has published several popular novels including the Alien People Chronicles sci-fi adventure trilogy (Alien People, Dark Metamorphosis, Among Hidden Stars). Sign up for his author newsletter Strange New Worlds, to satisfy your cravings for original stories, poems, and articles.

Praise for Alien People

★★★★★

"With lovable characters and plenty of suspenseful action sequences throughout, this is definitely one captivating sci-fi ride you don't want to miss out on. Kudos to John for crafting such an intriguing adventure!"

Meet AJ Pagan IV

Yes. You did it. You read this ridiculous story. Thank you. Thank you. Thank you. This is a satire, this is a joke, this is as dumb of a story as I could ever create. And it was fun as all heck writing it. I must say, I have never even thought of writing anything comical, but Phillip Carter inspired me. Thank you, you beautiful bitch. This story, AND THE CAT'S DEAD, RIGHT?! is and was a writing experiment, much like the thought experiment about a cat in a box. Did I do Schrödinger justice? Probably not, but it was fun to write, and hey, let's face it, if you got this far, you either enjoyed it or are as dumb as Brad for still reading. Why are you still reading? This story is over.

Praise for Brian, Created Intelligence

★★★★★

"A. J. Pagan IV has the ability to make the future scary. Using what we know about our lives today and projecting us into a freighting future for humankind. I recommend this story to all those who enjoy espionage and science fiction."

Meet Robin Drown

Robin is currently 150,000 words deep into a 2,000,000-word prison sentence imposed upon him by the High Church-Court of Penal Literature in Wigan. As an act of rebellion, he wastes these letter-constructs on multigenre stories, making his stories inaccessible to anyone with a solid brain. Sure, you might like sci-fi and you might like fantasy, but what if somebody poured horror and comedy gravy all over your genre steaks? Nobody likes that, do they, Gavin? In Drown's Reymouth Trilogy, Claire Pierce - a young, successful, irritable and easily distracted businesswoman - is forced to return to the seaside town she has been avoiding since childhood. For her, it has always been a place for heartbreak and isolation, but now something darker still is approaching. A ghost, a demon, a stalker, or some combination of the three? Join her in Seagulls and Seances to find out.

Drown has never been to space but he would choose to go during the day so he could get a better view.

Praise for Misery Breaks

★★★★★

"It will take your mind to places it doesn't want to go and didn't know existed, but on your return you'll be glad you went there."

Meet Phillip Carter

Phillip Carter is a comedian, science fiction author, poet, and Lego artist. To witness all of these weird things, sometimes at the same time, check out whobuiltthehumans.com. Alternatively, you can stalk him online by searching for RealPhillipCarter.

His debut book, Who Built The Humans? is a hilarious, manic multiverse heavy with existentialist musings and lightning-fast jokes. It's some freak hybrid of anthology and novel, a novelthology where eleven universes scramble to answer that strange question that forms the book's title.

Praise for Who Built The Humans?

★★★★★

"Whether you're into Douglas Adams or Isaac Asimov or Robert Heinlein, there's something in here for you."

★★★★★

"An astonishing creation, filled with conjecture and supposition. I can honestly say that I have never read anything like this before. The scope is Universe wide and simultaneously microscopically small and incredibly intense. [Phillip] infuses the book with an acerbic devastatingly acidic wit compounded with a bone-dry sense of humour."

The bit after the end

It is now the end of the book, so you should probably return to your life now or something. But this is not the end of all the books, because there will be more books probably. I don't know, I haven't been to the future to check.

If you want to read more weird stories, consider subscribing to our free newsletter, Halfplanetpress.substack.com, where we find and distribute free books and stories, usually Science Fiction and Comedy.